THE FOURTH LEVEL

OUTLAW

BOOK FOUR

I0544347

NICHOLAS HUNTLEY

First Edition, February 2018

nichhuntley.ca

WHITEWOLF PUBLISHING

Paperback ISBN 978-1-988765-01-3

Digital ISBN 978-1-988765-00-6

The text of this book is set in Times New Roman.

"The first symptom of love in a young man is timidity; in a young girl, boldness."

– Victor Hugo

Act 1, Scene 1

A heavy downpour roared down on the dirtied streets where litter accumulated along the flood gates and floated into potholes along the roads. A dark reflection of the surrounding slums could be seen against the oil slicks of the cracked streets. Electrical wiring drifted above, going from building to building. The homeless and lost lumbered along the sidewalks like zombies. The roadside shops had either cracked or barred windows with little entrances into the cramped rooms where cheap oriental restaurants, self-serve laundromats, and shady pawn shops existed.

A public tramline bus passed along the street with its wires coiled into the power lines above. The entire city street was lit in a warm orange tone. A cheap grey sedan of the last century parked on the curb. Inside the car was a man in a dirty brown army jacket. He leaned against the driver's seat window and smoked a cigarette – a hereditary habit that contributed to the disfigurement of his otherwise young face. The man had pepper-black hair and a stubble along his face with ears that pointed out. His skin was pale and he had a deviated septum. He tapped his cigarette and let the ashes fall to the ground before raising it back to his mouth for another inhale. The man was dressed in ripped cargo pants and heavy boots. He also wore a stained white shirt underneath his jacket. His eyes were focused outside and towards the consignment store where another man was hassling a shop owner.

The man was a stocky character with tattoos along his forearm, a khaki jacket atop his wife beater and torn blue jeans. He had brown hair and a nub where his upper arm used to be. The man argued with the old Chinese foreigner on the other side of the counter before grabbing the cash in spite and shoving the door open. The man then walked towards the grey sedan parked along the curb. The black-haired man quickly put out his cigarette, pushing it against the decaying grey paint of the car before placing his hand on the steering wheel and starting the car. The brown-haired man opened the passenger seat door and sat inside.

"How'd it go?" the black-haired man asked.

"Terrible," the brown-haired man replied. "Just drive."

The brown-haired man took a wad of cash from his jacket and counted it with the additional amount he had just acquired. The black-haired man started to drive off.

"I don't know what's going on with these people," the brown-haired man said, putting the money back into his jacket. "Scot is going to have our balls for this, this time."

"How much do we have?" the black-haired man asked in an anxious tone.

The car pulled into a gravel road near a shipping warehouse along a large river – Harlech River.

"Not enough," the brown-haired man answered. "He's gonna kill us for sure."

"If they kill us, then who's going to fetch their money?" the other replied, tapping his head. "Think about it."

The car drove to the end of the road and shined its lights to a man in a formal black coat, waiting patiently in the rain.

"Yeah, I'll think about that when he lines us against the wall," the brown-haired man said as the car stopped.

"Here, give me the bills," the black-haired man said, taking the cash from his hands.

The black-haired man took out a twenty-dollar bill and hid it in the car.

"What're you doing? Are you insane?"

"If they're going to punish us, may as well pay for my drinks," the black-haired man reasoned. "Come on."

The two of them stepped out of the car and walked towards the man. The car engine and lights stayed on. The appearance of the man in the coat became easier to see as they got closer. He was older than both of the others, clean-shaven, and had very fair skin. He had a brooding appearance and thick eyebrows.

"Good evening, Mr. Cambridge and Mr. Morris," the man greeted in a Scottish accent. "You lads better be having my money this time around."

The man took out his hands from his coat and accepted the cash into his hands.

"This is thin," the man said. "I don't like it."

The other two men looked at each other before watching the other count it before putting it away. He then looked to them with disappointment.

"You're short by about a thousand dollars, gentlemen," the suited man replied, brushing his coat open to put a hand on the pistol on his belt. "Do either of you care to explain yourselves?"

"We're sorry," the black-haired man replied. "We didn't steal any of it, I swear. The owners in our portfolio are all complaining of slow business. They're just not making enough cash to pay us."

"Then let me explain to you how it's supposed to work," the man replied. "You," he said, pointing to the brown-haired man, "are supposed to intimidate them while you," he pointed to the black-haired man, "are supposed to put that no good mouth of yours to use and talk to them. With the right motivation, there should always be enough if not more. Understood?"

The others didn't reply.

"So, here's what I expect from you next time," the man said to them. "I want your usual amount plus what you owe me by the next time we meet. Got it?"

"What?!" the black-haired man questioned. "How can you expect us to get that much? Are you nuts?!"

"I think you might want to be careful with the way you speak to me," the suited-man replied, walking towards him. "Do you see Felix here with his missing arm? Do you want to be like your friend here? Armless? Because if I don't get my money by next week, then I'll have to arrange to have yours amputated too, Willis. Do I make myself clear?"

"Please," Willis remarked. "Don't hurt me."

The suited-man shook his head.

"You're a pathetic man," the man replied taking a step back before walking away. "Get your job done or face the consequences. Oh," he added, turning around to face them once more. "And if for any reason I'm able to even suspect that you've been stealing from us, Cambridge, you're done."

The man walked off after these words and disappeared around the corner of the warehouse.

"*Do I make myself clear, Willis?*" Willis said, mocking the suited-man's accent. "What an idiot. Come on, let's go."

The two of them returned to the car and sat down.

"Nice job," Felix sarcastically remarked. "We're dead for sure. He knows you stole from him."

"Shut up, you faggot," Willis replied. "I'm tired of these idiots. Let's drink."

"Drink? After all this, you want to go drink?" Felix questioned. "Take me home – you can go get drunk on your own as usual. I'm done."

"You wimp," Willis replied, pulling out. "Some friend you are."

"I'm not your friend, Willis," Felix said. "I'm your unfortunate partner in this crappy job."

"Oh, shut up."

Willis drove his partner home before he drove off to a liquor store. He returned to his car with a pack of beer in his hands and tossed it into the passenger seat. He opened one and started to drink as he went home to his own apartment. The brick building he lived in was about four-stories in height with an alleyway on its right. A fire escape was lined against the side of the apartment from the top of the building to the second floor. The man parked his car in said alleyway before walking down to the sidewalk to get to the main entrance. He entered the building to embrace the smell of exotic herbs and spices and trudged up the stairwell in his drunken state from the lobby to the fifth floor. He then pushed against the patched wooden door ahead of him, opening it in a loud creak before limping along, but stopping at the corner as a brown bottle was thrown to the wall next to him.

"Where the hell have you been?!" a woman shouted from the kitchen around the corner. "You told me you would be back in twenty minutes eight hours ago!"

"I said I was going to work, you psychotic bitch!" Willis replied, raising his hands up as he walked into the kitchen before lowering them.

The woman in the kitchen had light brown hair and a slim figure. She was as young as her husband with blue eyes and fair skin.

"Oh, you were 'working?' Please, do tell me you have money then so we can feed our daughter," the woman sassed at him. "Or money so that we can clothe her and get some diapers."

"No," the man laughed at her. "The Feds give you three-hundred dollars and you want more? You really are crazy."

Willis started to walk away from her.

"I'm talking to you," the woman snarled.

"What do you want?" Willis questioned, raising his hands up. "I told you that I don't have any money!"

"You deadbeat!" the woman cursed, throwing a fork at him. "You useless waste of space! What good are you?!"

"Get off my back, you bitch!"

"Why can't you care for your own daughter?! Why don't you go out and earn an honest dollar to support this family?!"

"I never wanted a family!" the man remarked. "I told you to abort the little parasite because I knew this would happen!"

"Do not call her that!" the woman replied, throwing more utensils at her husband. "You do not call my little angel a 'parasite' -- you do not reduce my sweet Diana like that!"

The two adults continued to fight in the kitchen as the eleven-month year old looked on from where she was sat on the living room carpet. The lights of the TV flashed against the sides of her face as she gave a confused look to the man and woman fighting before turning back to the TV. She was dressed in only a diaper and the pacifier in her mouth. Her curious eyes looked to the TV where it showed a loving couple and their own child with smiles against their faces.

The little girl looked at the TV as she held a block in her hand before looking back to her own parents. The shouting in the apartment was obnoxious and loud, and yet she could understand and look on with a saddened face.

Act 1, Scene 2

"Cheers!" Tristan exclaimed, tapping his glass with Charlemagne's.

Diana, Tristan and Charlemagne were sat in a rustic restaurant in downtown Allabrese. The walls and floor were made of wooden panel. The entire restaurant was decorated with Western-theme decorations of the Wild West. The tables were draped with a checkered table cloth, and the lights created a warm atmosphere from the harsh late winter vibe outside.

Diana looked to her adoptive-father and adoptive-brother with a shy smile as they retracted their glasses.

"Come on, Diana," Tristan said to her with a smile. "Cheers."

Tristan slid his glass over to Diana's and tapped it. Charlemagne held a wide grin as he cleared his throat. Diana continued to spin the straw around in her strawberry lemonade.

"Anyways," Charlemagne said, "so there we were running out of the caves, and it turned out that one of our boys (the muscular one) had donned a minotaur costume and pranked us. I was livid, but we all had a good laugh about it for the rest of the trip."

"Wow," Tristan replied.

"Yes, that was one of the wilder adventures I had whilst in Greece, but it was also the most memorable. I would have to say that these were peak days of Cabernet Exploration up to when we could no longer support it. You know, half of the exhibits in the Royal Harlech Museum came from the contributions we had made. The problem, however, was that our historical and archeological research did not yield much of a profit."

"So, what happened?" Tristan asked.

"Well, once the company had to stop funding us, I decided to put my own funds into financing trips. However, we had to still make cutbacks so we couldn't handle such a boisterous team. And then there were other issues, of course, so despite these last expeditions, there was a clear sentiment that these would be our *last* expeditions."

"What a shame," Tristan said.

"Yes, it was a shame, Tristan," Charlemagne replied. "However, it was inevitable that this period in my life should have come to an end."

"Yeah."

"Anyways, there was a tribute to Cabernet Exploration in the entrance of the office, and it caused me to think about the good times as I walked in for my monthly meeting with the investors."

"Oh, how'd the meeting go?" Tristan asked.

"Well, we mostly discussed the security issues on-hand, especially since the robbery and tragic murder of a security team at Cabernet Laboratories last autumn. A series of new measures will be introduced, but none of them have considered the role of a mole in the company or which of our rival companies could be responsible for this infiltration. It was a boring meeting, but it took up most of my afternoon."

"Did they talk about what happened to us in Russia in December?" Tristan asked.

"No," Charlemagne replied, "none of that was brought up, mostly because nothing new has reached us regarding Yuri – I mean, Sergei Bykov since his court date isn't until next year."

"Wow," Tristan replied, turning to Diana and focusing on her as she looked to the side.

"Anyways, that was my day," Charlemagne sighed. "How was yours?"

"Oh, nothing exciting happened today," Tristan replied, turning back to his guardian. "All I had was a dissection lab in science class to brag about."

"How was lacrosse practice then?" Charlemagne questioned.

"It was good. Luckily, it was pretty sunny today so we weren't that miserable, but it was still hard to play with all the snow around."

"Well, we can expect that to last for another month or two," Charlemagne replied. "A bit of chill can be good for physical activity but do remember to not stay outside for too long. How about you, Diana? How was your day?"

Diana flinched and turned to her guardian. Tristan and Charlemagne were looking at her.

"Oh, uh... I don't know. I had school, and that was it..." Diana replied.

"Well, that's good – there's nothing shameful about a normal day. Sometimes, it can be good and needed," Charlemagne remarked with a pleasant smile.

Charlemagne continued to talk as he went into an anecdote about another one of his adventures. Diana didn't listen, however, and instead looked to the side. Tristan noticed a frown on her face as he listened to Charlemagne talk about his long adventure in Mongolia when he was twenty-two. Diana's attention resurfaced ten minutes later as she jumped as Charlemagne said her name.

"Sorry," Diana replied, "what were you saying?"

"I was saying that I hope the weather will pick up as it was today," Charlemagne repeated, taking a sip of his wine. "I talked to a colleague at work and he's agreed to let us come down to the Allabrese Equestrian Center to show off his horses and let us ride them."

"Horse riding? I haven't done that in ages!" Tristan replied, smiling.

"Yes, it's about time that we do something outdoors," Charlemagne remarked, "and it's also about time that I give you kids a taste of the countryside that Allabrese is known for. You know, the manor was once the home of several horses back in the day – before I turned the stables into a garage to park vehicles. My grandfather owned horses, and it was one of the few activities he and my father both bonded over, other than I suppose camping, which explains why my father was quite the rancher before he left with my mother on their humanitarian adventures."

"How come we never hear about your parents?" Tristan asked.

Diana turned to look to Charlemagne as he took a deep breath.

"Well, it's because they're both retired recluses that have vowed to disconnect themselves from mainstream society. When the two met, they were young – about your age. My grandparents (his parents) had to raise me in Allabrese when he was in high school, and then when he graduated, instead of going to college, the pair travelled the world while my grandparents were supposed to be enjoying their retirement. The two of them didn't stop travelling until Allodia was born, and since Salmar turned eighteen, they've been picking up where they left off."

"Will we ever get to meet them?" Tristan questioned.

"Oh, perhaps one day, but truth be told, I haven't seen them in years. However, Allodia did mention to me that they turned up in Harlech once upon a time last year."

"Can you imagine that?" Diana said to Tristan. "Charlemagne's parents."

"Yes," Charlemagne laughed. "Since they were both sixteen when I was born, that's the age gap between us. They're not much older than me."

Tristan smiled to Diana before glancing over to their waitress as she brought over their food. The three of them ate before Charlemagne paid the tab. They then left and returned to the black sedan parked behind the restaurant. Charlemagne went to the driver's seat while Diana and Tristan went to the seats in the back.

Charlemagne started the car and pulled out to the road. Diana looked out her window and towards downtown Allabrese as they drove off. The car passed central park and city hall before passing in front of the police department and courthouse as they drove towards the river.

The February evening was quiet and dark, especially along the road leading back to the mansion. The car passed by the Dawson Estate and then all the ranches along the banks of the river in what was St. Allan's Plains on the west-side of town before driving over the bridge.

Charlemagne pulled into the manor driveway once the automatic gates opened up to grant them access. The sedan pulled along the stone causeway, stopped atop the hill and shut off. The three of them got out of the car and walked up the steps to the front door of the house. Charlemagne took his keys from his pocket and opened the front door before they stepped into the dark house. Charlemagne was sure to turn on a lamp before he took off his coat.

Tristan closed the door behind them before he removed his jacket. Diana didn't bother to remove her jacket and instead went up the right staircase to go upstairs. Tristan watched her disappear before he looked over to Charlemagne.

"I'll be in my study for about an hour," Charlemagne said to Tristan. "If I don't see you again tonight, goodnight."

"Yeah, goodnight, Charles," Tristan replied, watching him go towards the library before he went upstairs.

Diana hurried down the hallway back to her room, entered, and then closed the door behind her. Her room was dark, so she walked over to turn the lamp on her desk on. She then took off her black jacket and put it in her closet. She then grabbed her red hoodie and put it on. She then jumped as she heard a knock on her door.

"What is it?" Diana asked.

The door opened and there was Tristan. He held his jacket on his forearm and looked to her. Tristan's hair was neatly trimmed since the trip to Russia and it seemed as though he had grown an inch. He wore a black sweater with a dark red shirt underneath and dark blue jeans. Diana was dressed in a black shirt and had light grey jeans on. Her dark-brown hair was a fair length and tied in a ponytail.

"What do you want?" she asked.

"What's up?" he replied.

"Nothing," Diana said to him, taking a last sigh. "I'm fine. Why would I be any different?"

"I don't know," Tristan shrugged. "Tired?"

"I'm always tired," she said, smiling.

Tristan gave a warm smile to her. He then stepped forward and closed the door behind him. He then walked over to her.

"What are you doing?" Diana questioned him.

"I-" Tristan paused for a moment. "Diana..."

Tristan paused again. His cheeks were red and his hands were trembling. Diana continued to look at him curiously with her blue eyes

"What is it?" Diana asked in soft tone.

"Nothing," Tristan lied, stepping back. "I lost my train of thought and forgot."

"Oh... okay then," Diana replied.

Tristan turned around and left. Diana looked out her door for a minute after he had left before she walked over and closed it. Tristan hurried back to his room and entered it. He then closed the door and leaned against it.

"*Nothing*," Tristan mocked himself. "You idiot."

Tristan pushed himself to stand and then walked over to his dresser. He took out some gym shorts and a t-shirt for him to get changed into. He quickly did so before he walked into the home gym to sit down at a bench, lie back and grabbed the bar to do some bench presses.

Diana looked at her schoolwork on her desk and drew a heart around where she had written 'D + T.' She then closed her eyes and ripped out the page from her English notebook and threw it into the bin next to her. She closed her notebook and leaned back into her chair. She maintained a dismal look on her face and her lips trembled. She brought a hand to her forehead and looked down.

Five minutes later, she stood up and left her room to go downstairs. She entered the kitchen and took the elevator to the garage, but instead went into the cellar to be alone. She stood in front of her usual spot, which consisted of a lounge chair. However, her eyes fixated upon something new in the basement that had recently been brought in. It was the model of King Island that was formerly in Charlemagne's study last summer. Diana walked towards it and stood over it. She took a deep breath as she looked at it all.

"What I would give to go back," Diana mumbled. "I don't belong here."

Tristan returned to his room after working out and taking a shower. He then lay on his bed and looked to the ceiling for several minutes. He lay atop his bed, in his blue soccer sweatpants alone and his gold chain necklace around his neck. He rubbed his neck with a sad face before he dug underneath the covers and brought them up to his shoulder. He then closed his eyes and gave in to the night with sadness in his heart.

Act 1, Scene 3

A young girl in a red hoodie ran down a long alleyway as she held a brown paper bag in one hand and a fake pistol in the other. The sounds of sirens followed in the background as she rushed along to make her escape from the police behind her. It was night and there were only the lights of the sirens flashing behind her.

Laundry wires were stretched across above from building to building. The clouds above were extremely dark and brought down a torrential rain. The girl ran and ran, but they alleyway only seemed to get longer as if she were running on a treadmill. However, the objects around her – from the dumpsters, parked cars and graffiti on the walls passed along, which created a sense of motion.

The girl turned around to look behind her to see the police in the distance. The German Shepherds foamed at the mouth as they pulled on their leashes and ran for her. She then looked ahead and saw a dumpster underneath a fire escape. She climbed up the trash cans and then up onto the dumpster to climb over the fire escape railing. The dogs had reached her and snapped at her with their vicious jaws. She managed to escape them as she climbed over and started to make her ascent up the ladder stairs. She made it to the roof of the building and proceeded to run, jumping onto the roof next door and rolling on her landing. She stood up to continue running but tripped on the edge of a ceiling window and came crashing into the glass. She fell to the floor below, which consisted of some unstable wooden planks that broke for her to fall to the very bottom of the building.

The room around the girl was dark. She lay on the ground on her side and began to bring herself up slowly. She then looked around as she heard the sound of a woman crying in the distance. She found a door out of the empty room she was in and opened it to step into a hallway. She then looked around at the doors ahead and started to walk to the very end of the corridor. She opened the door and stepped inside into the empty room where there was only a fireplace providing light.

The crying intensified and came from a woman lying on the ground in front of the fireplace. The floorboards creaked as the girl walked over to the woman and dropped to her knees. The woman was screaming in pain and tears surfaced on the face of the little girl. The girl brought her hands to the side of the woman and started to shake her.

"Mom?" the girl questioned. "Mom, it's me."

The woman had stopped crying and instead had her eyes closed. She moaned as the girl nudged her.

"I'm sorry mom, but I lost the money. I got it, but I lost it trying to get back. I'm sorry...."

"Diana..." the woman moaned.

"Don't say anything, mom," Diana replied, standing up and coming around to kneel in front of the woman.

Diana moved the woman's arms so that she could keep her airway clear and also so that her knee and elbow supported her on her side.

"Stay here," Diana said to her mom. "I'm going to go try again and get us some money, okay?"

"I love you, sweetie..." the woman said in her sleep.

"I love you too, mom," Diana replied, brushing tears from her own face.

Diana stood up and walked into the foyer of the building. She then opened the front door and left. She found herself on the cold streets where it was still raining. She walked down the center of the empty street, keeping a distance between her and the various strangers on the sidewalk. She began to realize that they were looking at her, which caused her to stagger as she walked until she started to run.

The strangers on the street stopped walking and instead they all looking to Diana as she ran. She sprinted down the street and began to notice them walking forward and towards her. Soon, Diana was slowly becoming surrounded. She stopped running and looked around her.

"No," Diana shouted.

The people started to grab her.

"No!" Diana shouted again, waking up and leaning forward in bed.

Diana breathed heavily and had a terrible sweat across her face and chest. She looked around her room and calmed down. She pushed her bed sheets forward and brought her knees to her chest. She brushed her hair with her hands and brought it all around her neck to keep close. She also moved herself to the corner of her bedroom and propped her pillow behind her so that she could sit in comfort

Tristan lay on his side in his room, having heard the moaning come from Diana's room. His eyes were wide open and he had a frown on his face. He pulled his phone out from under his bed and looked at the time. It was almost three in the morning. He stayed awake for about twenty minutes, which was the same twenty minutes Diana took before she decided to lie back in bed and bring the covers over her.

At approximately five o'clock in the morning, Diana woke up and lay in bed for about an hour until she grabbed her book and read for another hour. By seven o'clock, she decided to go to the washroom and then downstairs.

Charlemagne was in the kitchen when she showed up and joined him. He was fully dressed and spreading butter on some toast.

"Good morning," Charlemagne greeted. "I'm surprised I beat you here this morning. How did you sleep?"

"Okay," Diana simply replied, shrugging.

Act 1, Scene 4

Charlemagne pulled his sedan into the parking lot of the Allabrese Equestrian Center and parked it there. The three of them then got out and walked towards a dirt path that led around to the fenced pasture along the side of the sports center. By the fence along the path was Charlemagne's colleague in a blue winter coat and jeans. He was a tall man, about six feet and two inches with fair skin that was identical to Diana's. He had dark-brown hair that was trimmed and green eyes. He was also a handsome, muscular figure and clean-shaven.

Diana looked around as they approached him. The grassland was short and wet around them, and there was still a lot of snow around.

"Howdy," the man greeted to them. "I'm glad you could make it."

"Hello, Audric," Charlemagne replied, shaking his hand before looking to the kids. "Children, this is Audric Zimmerman. He's a Board Director with Cabernet Industries and one of our investors. Audric, these are my children, Diana and Tristan."

"Hello there," Audric greeted. "How're you doing?"

"Hi," Tristan replied.

Diana didn't greet Mr. Zimmerman and he took notice. The two looked at each other for a split second before Zimmerman looked to Charlemagne.

"Come on, I won't keep you waiting any longer," Zimmerman said, slapping the top of the fence. "Prepare yourselves to see the finest racing horses you've ever seen."

Zimmerman led them down the path and towards a gate. They then walked into the pasture and came to the side of the equestrian center where they entered through the open doors to enter a spacious room that was like mechanic's garage, but for horses.

"Look ahead," Zimmerman said, pointing to three horses being groomed by some workers. "Charles, your father would be astonished at these three fine specimens. If it weren't for him, this town wouldn't have the passion for horses like he did."

"Yes, that was my father... 'passionate,'" Charlemagne replied with slight sarcasm.

"Of course, if it wasn't for that Jew, Cohen, this entire center would be in much better hands," Zimmerman added.

"Let's not be anti-Semitic," Charlemagne warned him. "What's in the past is in the past."

"No anti-Semitism here, Charles," Zimmerman replied. "After all, I'm a member of the tribe, so I'm allowed to take some shots at my own people."

Charlemagne didn't reply. Diana looked at the three horses. One of them had white hair and a brown coat, the other had a dark brown coat with black hair, and the last had light brown hide and white hair.

"My point, however, Charles is that your father is a respected man around these parts," Zimmerman continued. "It's important to have a father that cares... not that a child without one can't fair out in the larger world."

"Amen," Diana muttered.

Tristan flinched and was silent with all the talking.

"What kind of a man was your father?" Charlemagne questioned.

"I didn't have one," Zimmerman replied. "He abandoned my mother and me before I was born."

"I'm so sorry to hear that," Charlemagne said to him.

"Don't be," Zimmerman responded, looking to Tristan with a serious face. "It's water under the bridge..."

Zimmerman's eyes then went to Diana. He smiled at her.

"Anyways, it's not Father's Day so enough talk about our dads. "You're here to ride horses and not hear me make rude comments."

"Your horses are beautiful," Tristan said to Zimmerman. "I especially like that one."

Tristan pointed to the horse with white hair and a brown coat.

"My dad used to take me to the police stables where they had a horse just like that one," Tristan said.

"Is that so?" Zimmerman replied, looking to Tristan.

"Yeah," Tristan smiled. "Her name was Becky and we loved her! I used to take her for rides every summer!"

"Wait, you know how to ride horses?" Diana questioned him.

"Of course I do," Tristan replied. "I was raised in this environment."

"Children," Charlemagne said, looking to them. "Pay attention because we're going to be readying you up so we can ride along the Allabresian Trail."

"How exciting," Diana sarcastically remarked.

"It's not supposed to be adventurous, genius," Tristan replied. "It's meant to be slow, thoughtful and relaxing."

Diana rolled her eyes and looked around the large metal barn. There were TVs on the walls which flashed with results from races across the globe. There were also bales of hay around, and open stables where there were horses being brushes, groomed, or washed by the various ranch hands. It was a busy room.

"Kids, you'll be riding Almond and Sistine," Zimmerman said to them. "They're both Thoroughbred horses and eager to stretch their legs."

Zimmerman walked over to the dark-brown horse with black hair and led it over to them. A worker came around to place a saddle atop of her.

"Hello," Charlemagne said to the light-brown horse.

"Sistine is getting a bit slow nowadays," Zimmerman remarked. "He'll have to retire sometime in the near future."

"Whoa, hey girl," Tristan said, patting Almond on the shoulder.

Almond was indifferent to Tristan touching her.

"Go ahead, Diana," Audric said to her. "Pet one. They're not aggressive, and you'll have to sit on one of them so it's better to take your pick."

Diana looked at him and then over to Charlemagne and Tristan as they touched one of the horses each. She walked over to Almond and tried to bring a hand to her hide, but the horse moved herself out of the way and gave a quiet huff. Diana brought her hand back without touching the horse and frowned. Both Audric and Tristan frowned in return as well as they looked to the horse as it faced away from Diana.

"Almond," Zimmerman scolded. "Don't be rude. I'm sorry, Diana, I don't know what's wrong with her."

"It's okay..." Diana whispered.

"Here, come and meet Lightning," Zimmerman said, bringing her over to the third horse. "I intended Charles to ride him because he's a harder horse, but it appears that Almond is having a bad day so we'll just have to make sure that you take it slow."

"I'll ride Almond," Tristan said. "I've ridden before – I can handle her."

"Alright then," Audric said, "let's get these horses saddled and find you some helmets."

The three of them were given helmets that fit them before they could mount their respective horses. Diana climbed onto Lightning with the help of Audric while Charlemagne and Tristan mounted their own horses with ease.

Tristan then looked over to Diana as he held the side of the horse's neck. He walked over to her whilst riding Almond and smiled to her.

"You've got to hold the reins," Tristan said to her, pointing at the reins.

"Okay, thanks...." Diana quietly replied.

"There you go," Tristan said, backing up.

"She can figure out herself," Audric remarked to Tristan. "Leave her alone."

"It's fine," Diana remarked to both of them.

Tristan looked to Audric and frowned at him. He walked off and left them alone.

"Alright, are we all ready?" Charlemagne questioned from his horse.

Charlemagne led them out of the barn and towards the pasture. They met Audric at the gates to the trail where he opened them. He then watched them off as they entered the forest. They were led down a narrow path with shrubs along the side and thin oak trees with budding leaves around them. Tristan turned around to look to Diana behind him before looking forward again.

"What the hell," Diana remarked to the horse as it stopped.

The horse started to shake its torso and head. Tristan quickly turned his neck around as he noticed that the lightning had stopped. He stopped his horse and started to go over to them. The horse then tilted back on its hind legs as it neighed.

"Whoa, girl!" Tristan shouted, backing away.

Diana held on and managed to stay in place as the horse came back to the ground. Lightning quickly dashed off and passed Almond and Sistine at an alarming pace with Diana holding on.

"Oh crap," Tristan cursed, kicking Almond to run after them.

Charlemagne and Tristan hurried their horses to go after Diana. She held onto her horse as it raced along the trail. At a turn, it instead jumped over the bushes and rushed through the forest to reach a small hillock. The horse came to the top before going down to the bottom where it reared again.

Diana fell onto the ground as the horse neighed. It then came back to the ground and walked over to a patch of tall grass exposed through the snow to eat. She looked at the horse in shock, but before she could stand up the two looked up and over to the arrival of another horse jumping over the bushes in front of them.

The horse shouted at them in a deep neigh with a huff in its breath. The horse had a black coat, black mane and deep black eyes. Lightning freaked out and reared at the black horse, but the horse was unintimidated and instead neighed at him. The horse ran off and left Diana alone with this aggressive horse which had turned its attention to him.

Diana looked over to the black horse as it started to rear at her too. It gave strong huffs at Diana who instead frowned at the horse rather than run off. She stood up and looked to the horse with an angered tone.

"Who are you trying to scare?!" Diana snapped at the horse as it continued to rear at him. "Did you think I'd be impressed with this tough guy act?"

The horse scoffed at her before neighing and backing up. It tapped its forward leg into the dirt and then reared at her again.

Diana continued to frown at him and stood her ground. The horse came back to the ground and looked to Diana.

The sound of galloping behind them caused the black horse to jerk its head up and then run off. Charlemagne and Tristan arrived on their horses to join Diana. Diana watched the other horse in awe as it ran off.

"Are you alright?" Charlemagne asked Diana.

"Yeah," Diana replied, looking in the direction the black horse went off. "A wild black stallion came out of nowhere and scared Lightning off."

"I saw it, but where did Lightning go?" Charlemagne questioned.

"He freaked out and left," Diana replied, looking over to Charlemagne. "He went this way."

Diana pointed to where she had seen Lightning go off to.

"Strange," Charlemagne said, looking forward. "We better go find her."

"Here, climb up," Tristan said to Diana, offering his hand.

Diana looked at him nervously and felt her cheeks redden. She grabbed his hand and was pulled up and onto Almond's back. Tristan then turned Almond around and began to bring her towards where Diana saw Lightning run off to. He had Almond run at a light pace, which forced Diana to put her arms around Tristan's waist.

The two returned to the trail where they stopped in front of Zimmerman. He was on a horse with Lightning in a lasso. Charlemagne joined them and smiled.

"Ah, good," Charlemagne remarked to Zimmerman. "You found her."

"Yes, I found her wandering around inside, trying to get back into her pen and whining like crazy. I came down to see if everything was alright, but I can see for myself that you three are alright in the least. What happened?"

Charlemagne explained that Lightning raced off with Diana, dropped her not too far from where they were, and was then spooked by a mysterious, but aggressive black horse.

"A black horse?" Audric questioned. "Hm, it could be that reckless wild horse that's been jumping into the enclosure and scaring the other horses."

Diana listened as they talked about the horse.

"Local horse-enthusiasts in town have been nuts about that horse," Audric explained. "Some of them want him gone, while others want to capture it for themselves. An outlaw like that is worth a lot to folks in the bronc riding business. The strangest part is that nobody knows where this beast came from. The poor thing seemed to have turned up just out of the blue!"

"Curious," Charlemagne replied.

The four of them rode back to the equestrian center. There, Charlemagne dismounted from Sistine and Zimmerman from his horse.

"You, uh... can let go of me now," Tristan said to Diana.

"Sorry," Diana replied, letting go and jumping off.

Audric and Charlemagne talked to each other whilst the workers removed the saddles from the horses and took them back to their pens. Diana and Tristan stood in awkward silence as the adults talked. Audric then turned over to the kids.

"How about it?" Zimmerman questioned them.

"Sorry, what?" Tristan asked, looking at them.

"I was just talking to Charles and we're wondering if you'd be interested in a pair of tickets to a local race next weekend. I think it'd be a great opportunity for the two of you to learn of the sacred traditions of this town."

"Oh, that sounds awesome!" Tristan replied, smiling to Audric before looking to Diana. "How about it?"

"Yeah, sure," Diana responded.

"Excellent," Audric said, "I'll get the tickets to Charlemagne and he can take you. I won't be able to attend as I've got travel to Harlech, but the local derby is known to be a hell of a goodtime."

"Good," Charlemagne said, nodding. "Let's go have some lunch now. I hear the restaurant here is still as good as it was back in day."

"Of course," Audric replied, "on me, of course."

Charlemagne and Zimmerman began to bicker over paying as they started to walk off. Tristan looked to Diana as she quietly walked behind them with her arms crossed. He walked over to walk next to her, and the two were silent as they walked.

Act 2, Scene 1

Moira looked over to Diana with slight pity and curiosity as she stirred the lone serving of apple sauce on her tray with her spoon.

"What's up, Diana?" Moira asked, looking at her apple sauce.

"Meh, nothing much," Diana replied, shrugging. "Why?"

"Why? Because it's almost been our entire lunch hour and you've still not even touched your food," she replied. "Also, you missed the track and field meeting upstairs after we both said we'd join together."

"Sorry, I'm not that hungry to be honest," Diana replied, continuing to play with her food. "Also, I've got cramps. I'm sorry that I missed the meeting."

"You wouldn't shut up about how much of a great sprinter you are, and now it's like you don't even want to join and show off," Moira complained.

"I have a lot on my mind," Diana sighed.

"Right, well, you're lucky it was just an information session and not the actual sign-up meeting," Moira replied. "I can just tell you later what was up... when you care."

"Cool," Diana replied, sighing.

The two went quiet for a minute before Diana slowed down her stirring.

"Can I ask you a question?" Diana expressed.

"Sure, what?" Moira replied.

"What's it like to grow up in a normal family?" Diana asked, looking to her friend.

"A normal family?" Moira questioned. "What do you define as 'normal' in this question?"

"You should know what I mean," Diana said, looking to her with a serious face. "I mean a normal family with a mom and a dad, some kids, maybe a family pet or two. There's a responsible father who's a breadwinner and there's a responsible mother who's the caretaker of the children and house. You know, the very basic foundation of civilization..."

"Oh," Moira responded. "Well, I don't know how to give an answer to that..."

"Just describe what your family is like," Diana requested.

"Well, my family isn't exactly like what you described. For example, my mom and dad have jobs, and they don't have a happy marriage.... Does a family like what you described even exist?"

"Of course it does!" Diana replied. "Tristan had it before his parents died. His friends Peter and Aaron have it, and it doesn't matter if the mother has a job – women are allowed to get jobs... as long as their primary concern is their kids."

"Peter Huxley shouldn't be a role-model," Moira remarked to her.

"I don't see why not? I mean, he's not that much of an asshole, but that might be because I never cross him or talk to him since he's a senior. Regardless, he's class president, gets good grades, and plays sports. Vivian... she's annoying, but she still participates in clubs and such. And last winter, their entire family went on vacation to Hawaii! Richard Huxley has accomplished a perfect family, so it does exist."

"Yeah, but..."

"And those defects in Peter and Vivian, they could just be due to external influences in mainstream cultural society – it's not as potent here in Allabrese like in Harlech, but it still exists."

"So, do you blame your addiction to cigarettes as an external influence?"

Diana didn't instantly reply.

"I never said that my family was normal. I grew up in the most dysfunctional home possible. You know this. My dad was a psychopath and my mom was an addict. We barely had enough money or enough food, and we had one bedroom in our apartment – it was a two-room apartment if you don't count the closet of a bathroom we had. And my parents… they were always fighting!"

Diana sighed.

"Sometimes… it seemed like my dad hated my mom and wanted to kill her. Somedays, it was like she would kill him."

"I'm sorry, Diana," Moira replied.

"Don't be," Diana quietly said to her, poking at her food again. "The two of them… they may have hated each other, but they still never divorced or even separated. I have to admire that – the two of them still relied on each other, my mom for my sake."

"Right," Moira responded. "Well, my parents are separated and it was hard on all of us. I can't compare to your family nor should this be a competition, but my home wasn't a pleasant place as it might seem when you come over. I'm not happy with my dad all the time, and I know it's because of their marital situation."

"If a marriage breaks down, it's the parent's fault," Diana replied. "It's up to both parents to put an equal effort into staying together for the sake of their children."

"You're being idealistic," Moira said to her.

"I'm stating what I intend to do," Diana responded. "When I get married, I'm going to find someone who understands this. I don't know if I'll ever have a career, but I know what I have to do when it comes to being a mother and wife, and you know what, I'll be the best damn mother and the best damn wife, and we'll have the best damn family on Earth!"

Moira sighed and shook her head at him.

"And you know what?" Diana continued to say. "I'll make sure to raise my kids in a way where they won't be able to get corrupted. I'll have so much passion for them..."

Diana paused for a moment.

"I just need to make sure I find a husband who could understand this too," Diana quietly said. "A man that can defend us, provide for us, and also be there to instruct our kids. I want a man who understands the dangers of mainstream culture because it affected my parents, and I won't let it affect my kids as well – I don't want there to be anymore suffering in my family."

"You can't stop suffering in the world," Moira complained.

"I know, but I can limit it," Diana replied. "I just need to find the right man to do this with. These are realistic expectations."

"You're being very utopian and ideal," Moira remarked. "Talking, especially about how the world *should* be isn't being a realist."

"I'm not taking about what *should* be," Diana replied. "I'm stating what I intend to do."

Moira shrugged at her. The two went quiet as Diana frowned at her. Diana tensed her shoulders and continued to poke at her food. She then gave a sigh and tossed her fork to the side. With a sad face, Diana stood up with her tray.

"Where are you going?" Moira questioned, standing up and watching Diana as she left.

Diana dumped her food in the compost trash and then left into the corridor. Tristan saw Diana cross past him and storm off. He stopped for a moment before walking to catch up to her with his gym bag strapped across his torso, but he stopped himself and instead turned around to see Moira sitting alone.

Tristan walked over to her and sat down across from her.

"What's with Diana?" Tristan questioned.

"What do you care?" Moira replied.

"She's my… friend," Tristan said to her. "Of course I care about her."

"Well, I'm afraid I can't help you because I don't know what her issue is either."

"Great," Tristan replied, standing up. "Thanks."

"You know, she's been like this all semester," Moira added to him. "At least, it's been getting worse, I think."

"What do you mean all semester?" Tristan replied.

"I mean, since the end of winter break," Moira clarified. "You know, when you guys got back from Russia?"

Tristan looked at her for a split moment and then left. He held a serious face as he left the cafeteria and came to the T-junction at the back of the school. He looked around for Diana but couldn't see her. All he could see were the other students chatting around and laughing. He went upstairs to check the hallways around there and then went to the basement to check around. He ended his search near the stairs that went up to the gym and quit when he burst into the male changeroom.

Tristan's gym bag was tossed onto the bench, and he quickly sat down. He brought his hands to his head, closed his eyes and tilted his head down. He took deep breaths and then tilted his head back. He took more slow deep breaths and then opened his eyes. Tristan then punched the locker in front of him, denting the metal with his knuckles before retracting it and shaking his fist. He walked over to the sinks and turned on the cool water. He started to run it underneath the water before glancing up to himself in the mirror.

Tristan's eyes were red and there was more darkness under his eyes than usual. Tristan finished running water under his hand, but as he touched his knuckles, he clenched his teeth.

"Dammit," Tristan remarked, walking over to his gym bag and grabbing it.

Tristan left the changeroom and went upstairs to enter the office.

•

After Diana had left Moira, she walked down the hall before turning to go up the stairs. She came to the second floor, turned and continued down the hall before turning again and then turning right into the library. The school library was small and consisted of only six bookshelves with tables behind them and in front. There was also a small counter where the checkout desk was. Diana passed the desk and went down to the tables in the rear. She dropped her backpack and jumped as she noticed someone else at the other side of the table.

The boy looked at her with a grim face. He had tanned skin like Tristan, but blue eyes instead of green. He also had dark black hair and fine eyebrows as well as a fine jawline. He wore a black sweater and a collared shirt underneath. It was untucked. He also wore tennis shoes and dark grey jeans. The boy was Arturo Medici. He glared at her and she glared back at him. He went back to writing with his pencil in his notebook as Diana took out her school books from her backpack and set them on the table. She looked at them and then decided to take her latest read out and delve into it.

Diana read for about five minutes until the five-minute warning bell went off.

"There you are," Moira remarked behind Diana.

Diana put her book down and stood up. She looked over to Moira as she walked over to her. Diana was unimpressed.

"What?" Diana questioned, annoyed.

"I asked you where you were going and you completely ignored me," Moira replied.

"Sorry, but I didn't hear you," Diana answered, turning back around to put her books into her backpack. "I'll see you in art class, okay?"

"Sure," Moira replied, walking with her friend down the book aisle.

The two left the library and Moira walked off to the right, but before Diana could turn left she felt something tap on her arm. Diana turned and saw Arturo standing in front of her. He was tapping her shoulder with her book.

"You left this behind," Arturo remarked in a quiet, but slightly deep voice.

Diana looked at him. He was about the same height as Tristan, which was about two inches from her height, five feet and ten inches at the moment to his height of six feet.

"Thank you," Diana replied, taking her copy of *The Brothers Karamazov*.

"That's an interesting book," Arturo remarked to her.

"It *is* an interesting book," Diana said to him.

"What's it about?"

"Well, it's about a lot of things," Diana responded, pulling a strand of her hair back, "but for the most part it's about morals and ethics and surrounds three brothers, the Karamazov brothers, all three of which have differing views, especially on the subject of their terrible father."

Diana stopped as she looked at Arturo who was looking at her as he listened.

"You like books?" Arturo questioned.

"Yeah, they're kind of my passion…" Diana replied. "I especially love classical novels – they're my favorite."

"What's your favorite book?" Arturo asked.

"*Crime and Punishment...*" Diana answered. "It's by the same author as this," she said, raising up her copy of *The Brothers Karamazov.* "I recently read it over last winter break, and it really vibrated with me."

"How so?"

"Well, there's another ethical debate in 'Crime and Punishment' and the novel basically surrounds people who commit crimes, or sins, and the punishment that ensues, which sometimes comes as a psychological burden. For example, the main character is a proud nihilist who believes he can be like God and take the life of a problematic old woman under the logic that more good can come from her dying, which justifies his murder quest. He later starts to drown in guilt until he abandons his proud ways and submits to God."

"Are you religious?" Arturo asked.

"Well, I- when I was in Harlech, I used to visit a large cathedral near where I lived, and I was baptized there as a Catholic. I'm not one to attend church, but I do think about the subject, especially the afterlife from time to time..."

"Yeah, me too," Arturo replied, sighing.

"Sorry, I didn't mean to... remind you of that or anything."

"Don't worry about it," Arturo replied as the second bell went off. "I know you didn't intend to."

"Anyways, I'll see you around," Diana said, walking past him.

"Yeah," Arturo replied before turning to her. "I'll see you around too..."

Diana entered her history class and sat down. She put her copy of *The Brothers Karamazov* away and then took out her books.

Act 2, Scene 2

Next Friday, Charlemagne drove Diana and Tristan from the manor back to Allabrese Equestrian Center along the south banks of the opposite side of the river. There was a light drizzle pouring down, and additional snow had managed to melt, but plenty still sat around.

Charlemagne pulled into the parking lot of the equestrian center where there was a mild crowd. He found parking in the back of the parking lot and stopped the car there.

"I can't remember the last time I was here for a race," Charlemagne remarked, taking off his seatbelt. "The last time I was here, I must have been twelve. I believe it was the summer before I left for preparatory school in Harlech."

"I've never seen a race before," Tristan acknowledged as he left the car. "We never had a place like this where I grew up."

"Well, don't get too fond of them," Charlemagne responded. "The sport has degenerated over the years and drawn the largest filth from Canada into equestrian centers like these across the country."

"What do you mean?" Tristan asked as the three of them started to walk over to the main entrance.

"I mean, there's a lot of corruption when it comes to the betting table and a lot of needles being thrown away in the stables. Of course, when it comes to Allabrese, there's one man responsible for all of it. If there's anybody in town that should be avoided, it's this man: Barnett Cohen."

Charlemagne opened the front door for the kids and then walked in behind them. The entrance of the equestrian center was loud and modern. The floor were black and shiny, and the center was decorated with plants and TV monitors at almost every possible open surface. In front of them was the reception desk, which was behind a panel of protected bullet proof glass. Charlemagne presented their tickets at the desk before they were returned with passes. Charlemagne took the passes and gave one to each of the kids before they walked over to the stairs that led to the viewing gallery.

Charlemagne's phone began to vibrate as they were halfway up the stairs. Charlemagne took out his phone and looked at it.

"Oh dear, it's Judith," Charlemagne remarked, reading the text messages. "I forgot I scheduled a meeting with her at the labs today…"

Charlemagne stopped walking and started to text. Diana and Tristan stopped about two steps ahead of him and looked to him. Charlemagne then looked to them as he put his phone away.

"I'm sorry, but I have some loose ends to tie up," Charlemagne said to them, taking out his wallet. "Here's about forty dollars."

Charlemagne passed Tristan the money.

"Buy yourselves some snacks, maybe a souvenir, and also a cab if I'm not here before the event ends," Charlemagne said to them. "Tristan, pay attention to your phone in case I message you an update. Take care, you two."

"Will do," Tristan replied, watching his guardian leave.

Tristan turned around and noticed that Diana was already up the steps. Tristan caught up to her.

"You hungry?" Tristan asked as he glanced over to the concession booths lined along the rear of the stadium.

Diana shrugged and then turned to him.

"Don't let me stop you from eating anything," she remarked to him, putting her hands in her pocket.

Tristan didn't reply and walked over to one of the many stalls. Diana followed and stayed close to him. He got himself some snacks before they went to take their seats.

Diana kept her hands in her pockets as she looked at all the people sitting down around her with an upset face. She then faced Tristan for a brief second, turning away from him as he looked at her. Diana began to frown. She looked to the racetrack in front of them and kept her eyes on the workers walking around.

Along the sides of the racetrack were a series of advertisements from various sponsors, most of which were local establishments within town. A couple of horses with their jockeys and managers began to cross the side of the track. The jockeys were dressed in colored uniforms and were short people. Behind each horse and jockey, or sometimes next to them, were other people, some in business suits, some looking like average citizens.

The entire racetrack was large and wide. The inside had an inner course. The outer course wasn't a perfect oval by geometric standards. The start of the course where the starting gates were was a straight track that merged with the oval track. Towards the left, the open barn doors going into the stables where the kids were last week could be barely seen.

Diana and Tristan waited about twenty minutes for the race to get ready. The seats around them soon filled up, but it wasn't quite a full house. Diana heard the mumbling of the announcer on a loud P.A. system but could barely hear him through the chatter of people around her.

The crowd soon quieted down. Diana looked around with confusion. Suddenly, a loud bell rang and the gates in front of them flew open with more than a dozen horses storming off and down the track.

The horses rode along with their jockeys atop of them, holding the reins in a cross with one hand and using the other to whip the sides of the horse violently. The jockeys were focused with their heads pointed forward, feet firm against the stirrups so that they were crouched. Each horse rode swiftly across the course and migrated to the inner perimeter of the racetrack.

"Hey, there's Almond!" Tristan shouted over the noise of people.

Diana continued to frown. She saw a man in a blue and white uniform riding atop of a familiar dark brown horse in the lead. Almost all of the other racers lagged behind in a large group with another two horses even further behind. She kept focus on the jockeys and then looked to the crowd around her.

People shouted at the horses at the top of their lungs. Diana began to hold her railing tightly. She began to breath at a moderate pace. The horses were almost at the end of the last corner when Tristan looked to her.

"I think they're doing jumping after this," Tristan said to her. "I promise it's more than just racing."

"Great," Diana sarcastically remarked.

The lead horse approached the finish line. Diana began to notice the inaudible mumbling of the announcer in the background. He spoke as if he had the microphone in his mouth. The shouts in the audience grew louder before climaxing as the brown horse crossed the finish line. The crowd cheered and clapped. Diana gave a sigh as the noise quieted down a little.

"And there you have it, folks, the P.A. announcer shouted in excitement. "Almond led by Mr. John Parker and sponsored by Audric Zimmerman has stolen the race with first place. "Goliath and Baxter come in second and third respectively…"

The screeches of a woman behind Diana and Tristan caused Tristan to flinch. Without a word, she relaxed her fists and stood up to leave. Tristan looked to her and stood up.

"Diana?" Tristan questioned.

Diana climbed up the stairs to the exit and entered the long corridor with all the concession stands. She looked around and then walked towards a set of stairs going back to the lobby.

"Daddy! We're going to be late!" a girl complained.

Diana looked forward and saw a girl with her father, walking towards her.,

"Please, Sandra!" the father pleaded. "Enough! Please, just shut up and keep up!"

Diana glared at the man and stopped in front of his path.

"Excuse me," he said as he approached her.

The man tried to walk around her, but Diana moved to bump into him.

"Excuse me!" he shouted again.

"How about you show your daughter some respect!" Diana yelled at the man.

"Excuse me?!" the man remarked.

"*Excuse me?!*" Diana mocked. "Grow a spine and be a better man!"

"Stay out of my family's business!"

The man started to walk past and towards Tristan who had stopped at the entrance to the viewing gallery. He watched as Diana picked up a rock from a plant nearby and threw it at the man, hitting him on the back of the head. The man quickly turned around and glared at her. She took a step back and ran off.

"Hey!" Tristan yelled, running after her.

Diana ignored him and walked down to the lobby. She then pushed against the front entrance doors and left the building. Tristan began to go down the stairs when he came across a mob of people that blocked him. Tristan took a step back to move out of the way and take another staircase.

"Excuse me!" a deep voice queried.

Tristan stopped and looked to him.

"Excuse me, little man," another shouted to him.

The crowd stopped and faced Tristan. They were all dressed in black coats with black fedoras. Most of the men were fairly stocky, and there was even a tough-looking woman in the crowd.

"Yes, you," an older one remarked to him in a Londoner accent, "my good sir. My friends and I are new to this town, but we have an understanding that the righteous Charlemagne de la Cabernet is known to live here. Is that correct?"

The man took off his hat as he spoke to him. He had grey hair that was combed and held back. He had a decent figure as well and wore a wedding ring. He looked thirty-years older than Charlemagne, however.

Tristan hesitated to answer and then shrugged.

"I think he lives here," Tristan replied.

"Good," the man responded, "and we were also informed that he would be here for the afternoon show. Is that correct?"

"I- I haven't seen him," Tristan answered.

"Well, that's quite alright because my interest is not in him specifically, but in his adopted daughter. You appear to be her age... do you know a Diana Cambridge?"

Tristan hesitated to answer again, but soon shook his head to him.

"Sorry, I've never heard that name in my life."

"Oh, no worries then," the man replied, examining Tristan before putting his hat back on. "Sorry for being a nuisance. Gentlemen, please make a way for our friend here."

The crowd of men cleared a path for Tristan to walk downstairs. They then continued up to the second floor while Tristan ran out of the building.

Act 2, Scene 3

Diana left the Allabrese Equestrian Center and made her way past the parking lot and towards the dirt path she walked on last weekend. It had stopped raining, but there was still a thickness in the sky of light grey clouds. She began to stutter her steps before she fell on one knee and into the mud before her. Tears were rolling down her cheeks, but she was not actively crying. She wiped them and stood up to lean against the fence. She then began to watch the horses in the pasture as they fed themselves on grass.

Diana's eyes then focused on a black horse that had just ridden atop of a hill ahead. It reared and spooked the other horses before it charged downhill and stopped at a clearing of grass. It turned and started to walk away, avoiding the grass.

"Same," Diana remarked at the horse.

Diana continued to watch the horses disperse before she started to climb the fence and enter the pasture. She crossed to the other side and came atop of the hill. She then looked down and towards the banks of the Nattau River ahead. From where she was, she could barely see the mansion up the river on the other side. However, her eyes were focused on the black horse drinking from the river. She took a step into some snow in front of her and it alerted the horse to her presence. The horse looked at her and the two stared at the each other.

Within a minute, the black horse backed up and disappeared into the forest.

"Hey, wait!" Diana yelled, running after the horse.

Diana came into the forest and began to follow the horse through the bushes. She got closer, but before she could reach him, she tripped on a root poking out from the ground and fell. Diana quickly got up again, but the horse was gone. Diana continued to walk forward, coming out of the forest and into a puddle of mud. She saw a ranch in the distance, but it looked mistreated and abandoned. The barn to the side of it was charred and ruined, and the glass windows of the house were shattered at some sides.

Diana's foot slipped as she stepped into the mud, and she fell onto her side and started to slide down the hill. She stood up at the bottom of the hill and saw that most of the mud had cleaned itself off as she slid down the snow. She was, however, wet and cold.

Diana fixed her hair before turning to the side and towards the river where she saw the black horse again. The horse simply looked at Diana. Diana moved slowly to face the horse before taking a step forward. The horse took a step back.

"What're you doing?" Diana questioned. "I'm trying to get close to you!"

The horse neighed at Diana's nagging and stomped its hooves. Diana took the chance to walk closer to the horse as it shook its head rhythmically side to side. Once Diana was about two meters from the horse, it pushed off from its hind legs and reared at her.

"Please, try harder," Diana replied, unimpressed. "I trademarked the defensive moves here. You can try that with the cowards, but not me."

The horse came down to the ground and neighed at her.

"What's your problem? What makes a horse this much of an ass?"

The horse gave a shrugged neigh at Diana before moving its head to the side to avoid eye contact. Diana took another step towards the horse and the two kept a meter distance between them.

"I bet life as a horse is so tough that you need to act like a complete asshole to compensate for it."

The horse stomped at her and then gave a long neigh.

"What?" Diana questioned, turning around to look at the abandoned ranch. "Is- is that your home?"

Diana held a saddened face before looking back to the horse. The horse didn't respond to her. She took a step back and decided to go walk towards the ranch. The horse then galloped past and stopped in front of her. It reared at her, causing Diana to raise an arm to protect herself.

"Stop that," Diana complained, still unimpressed.

The horse came back down on its legs and began to stamp its hooves into the mud.

"So, this is your home then," Diana replied. "All I wanted was a simple answer. It'd be nice if somebody gave me some answers around here."

The horse neighed.

"You know, I'm a survivor too," Diana said to the horse. "I was trapped in a burning building once before too. I got second-degree burns because of it right across this arm."

Diana raised up her right arm.

"I had to go to the hospital because of it, and it was the first and last time I ever trusted my dad with anything."

The horse stopped neighing and looked at Diana with careful and focused eyes.

"Well, I guess that gives you a reason to be grumpy, especially if you were burned and have burns. I know I was grumpy when I lived in Harlech – I was defensive too. Then again, how could I have been happy with who I was? I had a hopeless life with hopeless parents. What about you? Where are your... oh. Nevermind. I don't suppose there are other black horses out and about, so I guess that means they..."

The horse huffed.

"Yeah, mine are dead too…"

The horse neighed.

"It's not fair, but soon you begin to realize that life isn't fair in general. Even horses don't get it easy. Don't worry, I know how you feel. What happens to us is nothing more than a spin on the roulette table. Some of us win, others lose. Life is certainly meaningless and unfair. You understand that, I bet. You're not like the other horses. I like that…You don't prance around and eat grass like them – you stand your ground and fight. I was like that too. I didn't let anybody boss me around. I was my own woman, but then I was fished out and brought here."

The horse gave a brief neigh at him before nodding its head.

"Fate rolled the dice, and I lost the privilege to be where I was and instead live here, in a big house in the middle of nowhere with a billionaire and a guy like me. You wouldn't like him though. He's not like us. I like him though… a little too much. Nothing's been the same between us since I saved his life. I- I just don't know what's wrong with me anymore. I can't hold myself when I'm around him. I melt. I feel hurt. And he doesn't realize it. And that hurts me more. My biggest fear is that I'm hurting him too, but I can't help it. It's making me hate this place. It's making me hate living with him because I get anxious and my heart races. My stomach turns and I just have to get away from him because I start to remember – that night. I just want to go home. Life in Harlech wasn't that great, but at least I didn't have to put up with this. I don't even fit in here. Tristan does, but that's his problem. I feel so left out sometimes, not just at home but at school too."

The horse neighed at her before taking a step forward. It huffed at her.

"I bet you would be angry if somebody moved out a hundred miles from where you once were, or maybe you'd be happy about it – a fresh start, a new life. But then you'd find a beautiful mare and you'd drive yourself crazy over her to the point where you want to go back home. Then again, I suppose you could always just run away. I'm stuck here."

Diana paused and raised a hand to stroke the horse's forehead.

"I just realized that you're still here and not trying to scare me anymore," Diana remarked. "You know, you can't scare me. I faced a Yeti last year and *that* was scary."

Diana continued to stroke the horse along the forehead before brushing her hand along his face.

"You don't have to scare me. I won't hurt you. I won't let anyone hurt you. I understand you. I'm just like you. We'd be different people if it weren't for the circumstances we were put under, but we aren't those people. All we can do is hope to raise those people and be better than the people who raised us. I want to have a family one day, but since I'm not a man I can't really be the father I never had although I could be a mother I never had – not that I had a bad mom, but I suppose she could have been better and I can aim to be better. The important thing about all the suffering I've endured is that I have an intense ability to empathize. I bet you understand empathy too. That's why you're letting me touch you, because you trust me. Maybe we're still naïve and therefore fools for trusting each other, but I feel like we won't betray one another. I can feel the fire that still burns inside you – the fire that's changed you. It's unfair that we can't be in control of our lives and instead have to let the outside forces mold us. Not that it matters. Nothing matters. All we do is add meaning, and that makes room for delusion."

The horse calmly let Diana pet him while he listened. Diana took a deep breath and closed her eyes. She was breathing calmly. She opened her eyes and looked at the horse's black eyes.

"You're wild and mean. I'd name you 'Typhoon,' but that doesn't work with you. If you were a person, you'd be sarcastic all the time like me. I'm going to give you an ironic name. I'm going to call you 'Zephyr,' like a light gust instead of a mighty storm. You're just like me, Zephyr. I'm not really a typhoon and neither are you. We just act like one to defend ourselves because deep down, you and I are gentle and loving creatures. We're both light gusts, but that's just between the two of us, okay? Your name will only be sarcastic to other people, but to us, it'll have a true meaning."

"Diana?" Tristan shouted from behind.

Diana turned and looked to Tristan atop of the hill. He started to gently come down the hill, causing Zephyr to back away.

"No, don't worry," Diana remarked to Zephyr in a quiet tone. "He's just that idiot I was telling you about – the one I like."

Tristan stopped at the bottom of the hill and slowly walked towards them. Diana turned back to him.

"Hey," Diana greeted. "What's up?"

"What's up?" Tristan questioned. "I should ask you that. You ran off without saying anything to me, threw a rock at some dude, and then disappeared on me. What's wrong with you?"

"Nothing," Diana replied, gently petting Zephyr.

"Isn't that the horse from last week?"

"Yeah," Diana replied. "It's the same one. I saw him and thought I'd say 'Hi.'"

"Right," Tristan replied, looking back at the horse as it gave him a nasty look.

The horse neighed at Tristan. Tristan took a step back.

"This poor little horse," Diana remarked, rushing her hands over the horse's forehead. "I'm pretty sure he's from the barn over there. I think he must've been separated from his owners, or something."

"Okay?"

"Can we bring him back to the mansion? He's domesticated and needs a place to sleep. He'll die if he stays out here on his own – or worse, somebody will capture him."

"Are you nuts? Where are we supposed to keep a horse?"

"In the garage," Diana replied. "Charles said it used to be a stable."

Tristan looked to Diana with doubt.

"Please, Tristan," Diana pleaded. "You've got to help me."

Tristan sighed.

"Fine," he replied.

Act 2, Scene 4

Tristan returned to Diana with a rope, which he tied into a lasso so that Diana could lead Zephyr away from the abandoned ranch and down to the road. Tristan followed from behind, and the three of them walked all the way up the road and towards the bridge, which was about a three kilometer walk.

By the time they were at the bridge, Tristan took out his phone and saw that he had several missed text message from Charlemagne. He was asking him when he and Diana wanted to be picked up. He sighed and replied saying that the event was over and they're walking home. The three of them then crossed the bridge and came down around to the narrow road that went to the mansion. From there, they stopped in front of the gates.

"You know," Tristan said to Diana, "most people ask for a cat or a dog as a pet."

"Yeah, but that's cliché and boring," Diana replied, looking up the slope to the mansion.

The lights in the laboratory and dining room were on. There was also a lamp on in the foyer.

"You owe me for this," Tristan said, opening the driveway gate.

"Sure," Diana replied, "I'm in debt to you. Now go distract Charles while I take the horse to the garage. I'm going to go around and come in through the pen."

"Fine," Tristan replied, entering through the gate and closing it.

Tristan started to march up the hill.

"And Tristan?" Diana questioned, looking to him.

"What?" Tristan replied in a sharp tone.

"I really appreciate this," Diana said with a smile.

Tristan dropped his serious tone with surprise. Diana started to walk off with the horse before he could give a soft smile as he continued to walk up the hill. He made it to the top and took out his keys. He then started to unlock the door before opening it. Tristan's eyes immediately darted up as he saw Charlemagne with an old woman.

The woman wore a black cardigan, white blouse and a black skirt. The woman had curly and short white hair. She also had fair skin that was wrinkled and an aging, kind face. The two of them were coming down the left stairs from the south wing of the house.

"Tristan!" Charlemagne greeted. "Why didn't you text me? Where's Diana?"

"She's, uh… around," Tristan replied. "Who's this?"

"I'd like to introduce you to my former nanny and our new caretaker," Charlemagne remarked. "This is Mavis Quinn. She used to work for my grandfather, at our old home in England before coming to work here afterwards up until people stopped living here. I've convinced her to come out of retirement so that she could look after you and Diana."

"Hello, it's a pleasure to meet you," the old woman spoke in an English accent.

"Hi," Tristan replied.

"She'll be handling the cleaning, laundry, and cooking – the tedious chores that I won't be able to help with as I'm planning on leaving in June to go to Spain for a… research trip."

"Oh, and on that note, I better go and get supper started," Mavis said to Charlemagne. "Is the kitchen still this way?"

"Yes," Charlemagne replied, "do tell me if there's anything that needs to be bought. I'll see to it that there's money to buy groceries."

Charlemagne put a hand in his pocket as he watched Mavis walk off.

"Yes, she's a lovely woman," Charlemagne remarked.

"I didn't realize you were looking for someone to take care of us," Tristan replied. "Or that you were going to Spain."

"Well, it'll only be a couple of weeks, Tristan. I didn't want to leave you and Diana alone for too long, and I wasn't looking. I heard from her daughter, Tabitha Hughes – sorry, Rivers, that Mavis' husband had passed on and that she was depressed, so she had me hire her. She will board with us."

"Daughter? Mrs. Rivers?" Tristan questioned, referencing his English teacher.

"Yes."

"And where's she going to stay?"

"Oh, she'll be sleeping and living in the suite under the house," Charlemagne replied.

"There's a suite under the house?"

"It's behind the cellar before the garage," Charlemagne explained. "It's a one bedroom suite with a kitchenette and bathroom. It's her old room."

"Diana won't be happy about that…" Tristan muttered.

"Why's that?"

"Diana likes to hide in the cellar," Tristan explained. "She won't be happy if she's passing through to get to her suite."

"Oh, well, that'll be a darn shame," Charlemagne responded. "Speaking of Diana, where did you say she was?"

"Uh…"

Diana snuck along the side of the fencing around the house, catching a glimpse of the lights in the kitchen as she came to the side of the garage. She walked past and then came to the wooden fence of the pen. She climbed over and Zephyr hopped over, stamping his hooves into the mud and causing some to splash onto Diana.

"Great…" she remarked. "Come on."

Diana led Zephyr towards the garage doors. She left him for a moment so that she could enter through the open backdoor and open the garage doors to lead Zephyr inside. Once inside, she closed the doors behind him and brought him over to an empty stall.

"See, isn't this as spacious as I told you it would be?" Diana said to Zephyr. "I'll get you some hay, and then this'll be better than what you had before."

Zephyr stepped out of his stall and looked over to Diana as she disappeared up a ladder. Diana went to a pile of hay above the garage and found a pitchfork to drop some hay down. She dropped a whole bale and pushed it towards the stall.

"There you go," Diana said, taking off the lead around Zephyr's neck. "That should be enough hay to last you… well, however long."

Diana closed the gate behind them and then looked to Zephyr as he ate. She then looked at the turned over bucket and the empty trough in the stall. She pet Zephyr as he continued to eat. She picked up the bucket and left the stall to bring it to a faucet at the end of the garage. She turned the valve and had some water pour in. She then took the bucket and poured it into the trough.

"I don't know much about horses," Diana confessed, "but I do know somewhat the basics about keeping a pet. I'll do some reading and see what I can find about raising a horse. I think you guys like carrots and salt cubes. We don't have much salt, but there's some carrots upstairs. I'll get you some as a snack later. I'll make sure I can get everything you need, even if I have to steal it. I might live in a mansion, but I'm not actually that rich – or do I have any money at all."

The horse continued to eat. Diana continued to pat him before running her hands along the back of his head.

"You're safe here," Diana said. "Nobody is going to try and capture you or try to hurt you. I promise that and I'll make sure that you're fed so that you can be strong and mighty as you want to be. I'm not going to leave you... I know that you're not going to leave me either."

Diana gave a warm smile at the horse as it raised its head and turned to her. Zephyr began to move his body around before slouching down to lie on the ground. Diana sat down and rested her body against him as he lowered his head.

"I'm not going to hurt you," Diana said to the horse in a soft tone. "This is your home now. This place took me in, it can take you in too."

Zephyr and Diana continued to lie down until she began to notice that she was hungry. She opened her eyes and looked over to Zephyr asleep. She decided to stand up and climb over the gate to leave.

"I'll be back tomorrow, maybe later tonight," Diana whispered. "I also wake up early, so I'll see you in the early morning."

Diana dropped down and started to walk towards the ladder. She climbed up and then entered the storage closet behind the kitchen. From there, she entered the kitchen and opened the refrigerator. She inhaled the smell of roast beef in the oven, which caused her stomach to grumble. Diana found some carrots in the fridge but decided to leave them there for now. She left the kitchen and went straight to her room to open her laptop and do some research about horses.

Thirty minutes later, she dined downstairs and met Mavis. After dinner, Diana quickly went back upstairs to continue her research. Meanwhile, Tristan helped Mavis with cleaning the dishes before he went upstairs to work out. Afterwards, he walked into the bathroom and locked the door so that he could shower. When Tristan was finished, he opened the bathroom door going into the gym and crossed it with his hair still wet. He held a towel around his waist and came back to his room to get changed for bed. He dried himself and pulled up a pair of sweatpants.

Tristan then walked back to the bathroom to turn off the fan and unlock Diana's door. He paused for a moment after he unlocked it and held a fist behind the door with intent to knock. He then opened the fist and turned around to leave.

Diana turned off her computer and stood up. She entered the bathroom and closed the door leading to the gym so that she could get ready for bed. Afterwards, she climbed into bed and went to sleep. She shivered as she felt the coldness in her room causing her to hold her covers tightly around her.

Tristan laid down in his own bed to sleep. He hugged the pillow next to him as he closed his eyes. He then drifted into his sleep as Diana did in her own room.

Later that night, Tristan woke up with grogginess as he heard the depressed moans of Diana come from her bedroom. He leaned up and rubbed his eyes. He then pulled his feet out of bed and walked over to Diana's bedroom. He knocked on the door and brought his ear to the door.

"Diana? Tristan quietly questioned. "Diana?"

No response came. Tristan sighed and went back to his room. He sat down at his bed and turned on his phone. It was almost three o'clock. He brought a hand to his chest and closed his eyes. He felt his heart beating rapidly. He pressed against his chest before looking at his phone to look at pictures of Diana that he had saved.

Diana opened her eyes and breathed sharply. She pulled herself up and turned on a light. She looked around her room and saw that she was alone. She then brought a hand to her forehead to wipe the sweat from her head before grabbing a sweater to bring over her top. She then stood up and walked around her room. She walked over to her closet and closed it, and then she walked over to the shelf above her dresser. She looked at the various items there, including a framed photograph of her and Tristan. Next to this photo was the robot head she salvaged from Russia. Diana picked up what was next to it, which was her former box of cigarettes given to her by Tristan. She picked it up and pulled out one of the cigarettes that was still inside.

Afterwards, Diana walked over to her desk to find her lighter.

"Hello, old friend," Diana whispered, picking it up and then looking around.

Diana looked to the French window leading to her balcony, but then looked past and over to where Charlemagne's bedroom was. She turned around and entered the bathroom. She looked at the switch that turned on the fan, but then she looked to the window behind the bathtub. She walked over and opened the window, which caused a slam noise.

Tristan's head jerked to the left as he heard the noise. He turned off his phone and stood up. He hovered his hand over the door going into the gym, took a deep breath, and then opened it. He looked ahead of him and didn't see anyone in the bathroom. Tristan walked over to the door leading into the bathroom and saw the window open. He put a foot into the tub and looked outside, and noticed Diana on the roof of the garage, climbing up to the top. He quickly moved out of the way and sat down on the edge of the tub.

Diana took her lighter and lit the cigarette. She then inhaled and exhaled, blowing smoke up and towards the moon. Diana's body relaxed as she did so. She brought the cigarette back to her lips and then took another puff. Tristan could smell the smoke. He moved to reveal himself.

"What am I doing here?" Diana questioned.

Tristan stopped to listen.

"I hate it here. I have nothing in this place... I should just leave. I don't want this anymore. I just want to leave."

Diana tilted her head down in resignation. Tristan came back down to sit on the side of the tub and rest his head against the wall.

"It's all my fault," Diana whispered. "It's all my fault. I'm a failure. I'm a loss – a liability. I shouldn't even be alive. I don't want to be alive. I don't want to do this anymore – not with the memories that keep coming back. I can't do this anymore."

Diana put out her cigarette on the roof tiles. She then gave a sigh and brought her knees to her chest to hug them. She stopped talking and stayed where she was, looking out to the field and mountains beyond.

Tristan lowered his head. He whimpered and his eyes rolled a tear.

"Diana..." he muttered.

Diana held her own head down as she started to roll tears, except her tears progressed into crying while Tristan simply wiped his tears and stood up. He left the bathroom and went back to his bedroom, closing the door behind him. He looked out his own blinded window to see if he could see her, but he couldn't. He then heard a thud in the bathroom and quickly went to bed.

Tristan lay in bed on his back with his eyes looking up to the ceiling. He stayed like this as Diana returned to her bed and climbed inside. She then turned her body towards the wall and fell asleep. Tristan continued to lay on his back for another five minutes until he turned to his side and closed his eyes.

Act 3, Scene 1

Diana slouched over in her seat during English class while she scribbled in her notebook. Moira read a book next to her. Tristan sat in front of them, doing homework. Vivian and Maia sat in front of him. The class was silent for the last ten minutes of class.

After the bell went off, Mrs. Rivers stood up from her desk and began to pass tests back to her students. Tristan received his and put it away before leaving. Diana got ready to leave as hers came around. Mrs. Rivers left it on her table with the back facing up. Diana slowly picked up the paper and looked at the F marked atop. She frowned and put it away before leaving. She held this frown as she walked past the smiling kids around her.

Diana reached her locker and opened it to get ready for her next class. She picked up her science textbook and notebook and shoved them into her backpack before taking a step back. Diana bumped into somebody, causing her to turn and back away.

"Watch it!" Peter shouted to her, looking at her with his brown eyes.

Diana looked at Peter with a serious and pale tone. Peter's face dropped and he left without saying another word. Diana walked forward and towards her next class but stopped to enter the washroom.

Tristan watched what had happened and felt his body tense. Peter didn't say anything about it as he came to him outside of the female washroom. Tristan was with Aaron at his locker, and he joined them.

"What's up, bruh," Peter greeted to them.

"Nothing much," Tristan replied.

Diana walked to the sink and ran the faucet. She brought some water to her face and then looked to herself in the mirror.

She tensed a fist as she heard the obnoxious giggling of Vivian Huxley outside.

"Tristie!" Vivian squealed, coming over to Peter, Aaron and Tristan.

"Oh, hi," Tristan replied without much excitement.

"Are you excited for the Easter weekend?"

"Oh, definitely," Tristan replied with sarcasm.

"You know what's special about the first day of April?" Vivian questioned.

"No, what?" Tristan answered.

Diana listened.

"April Fool's Day?"

"No, silly. It's the anniversary of our first date," Vivian replied. "How could you forget?"

Diana frowned.

"We're not dating, Vivian," Tristan replied to her.

"Ouch, savage, Tristan," Aaron laughed.

Vivian frowned and crossed her arms.

"I know we're not," she replied, "and I wish that changed, but I understand you're busy with school and sports. I'm still your gal though, right?"

"Yeah, Trist," Peter said, "isn't she your gal?"

"Shut up, Peter," Vivian scolded. "Well, Tristie? Am I not?"

"No," Tristan sighed. "I mean, you are."

"So… why don't you ask me out on a date? We missed Valentine's Day, remember?"

"I was busy, sorry."

"Yeah, too busy with his other woman, Vi," Peter replied. "Isn't that right, Tristie? This dog's been unfaithful to my dear sister and sleeping with his sister, Vi. Don't you know the dangers of inbreeding?"

Peter slapped Tristan on the back of his head. He flicked his hand away and frowned.

"She's not my sister," Tristan replied. "We're not even related."

"You still spent Valentine's with her," Peter said to him.

"I did it for her benefit," Tristan sighed.

"Did she at least repay the favor?" Peter asked.

"Shut up," Tristan replied.

"Yeah, leave my Tristan alone," Vivian fretted. "Can't you boys give us some privacy? Stop bothering him. He loves his sister. That's cute."

Tristan groaned. The boys laughed.

"Whatever," Peter replied. "I'll see you lovebirds elsewhere. I'm out."

Peter walked off with Aaron, leaving Vivian and Tristan together.

"I'm sorry they're so rude to you," Vivian said to him.

"Yeah, okay," Tristan replied, walking off with her.

"Can we go on a date though, please?" Vivian questioned. "I can make it a double date."

Tristan sighed.

"Fine," Tristan replied.

"Thanks, Tristie," Vivian smiled, kissing him on the cheek. "I'll text you about it later today. See you!"

Tristan sighed and walked off as Vivian went downstairs. Meanwhile, Diana sat atop of the bathroom counter with a frown on her face. She turned to look at herself in the mirror and saw a tear roll down. The bell went off as she stood up. She wiped her tears and left the bathroom. She came downstairs and left the building and crossed the field. She came around the bleachers but slowed down as she saw someone behind them already.

Diana made her approach, but brought her guard down as she realized it was Arturo with headphones in his ears. Arturo looked at her and then stood up, lowering his headphone and picking up his backpack. He started to leave.

"Wait," Diana replied to him, "you don't have to leave. I'm not a snitch."

"It's not about snitching," Arturo replied, "it's about being alone."

Diana didn't reply. Instead, she walked over to him and grabbed his hand to stop him. Arturo raised his hand up as Diana felt the coarseness of his hands where there were scabs.

"What's wrong with your hands?"

"Nothing."

Diana grabbed his hand again and pulled up the sleeve of his wool coat. There was bandager around his wrist, tied up along the side with blood stains. Diana didn't reply as Arturo retracted his arm.

"Don't you tell anyone," Arturo threatened her before turning to leave again.

"Then stay," she replied to him.

Arturo stopped and turned around.

"If you don't want me to say anything, then please stay for a bit."

Arturo looked to her and then went over to the school. He shook his head and walked back over, tossing his backpack onto the concrete and raising his hands up.

"What do you want?" Arturo complained

"Why are you cutting yourself?" she questioned. "What's wrong with you?"

"What do you expect…" Arturo remarked.

Diana didn't respond. Arturo had a tear roll down his face.

"My parents are dead too, but I've never resorted to self-harm after the fact."

"Good for you," Arturo sarcastically responded.

"I mean, I hated my dad so it was okay that he left, but when it came to my mom, I loved her. I still miss her a lot, and everyday… it's hard."

Arturo crossed his arms as he looked to her.

"Yeah," he quietly replied, "it is hard."

Arturo sat down. Diana sat next to him.

"You know, every day I feel guilty about it," Diana said to him. "I don't know why she had to die, or if there was any reason behind her dying. It makes me question whether there's really any purpose or meaning to the world."

"I know what you mean."

"I feel like it was my fault because I could have stopped her from dying. I could have saved her, and then that makes me feel like it was *my* fault that she overdosed."

"Overdosed?" Arturo questioned.

"Yeah," Diana replied. "She overdosed on some heroine that was laced with fentanyl."

"Jesus…"

"Yeah."

"And your dad?"

"He died years before this. He was gunned down by some crooks that he owed money to. You might know them, they're called the Harlech Syndicate."

"Yeah, I do know them," Arturo replied. "I've heard of them from my family. My *nonno* (grandfather) claimed they were the reason we lost our banking business back in the day."

"Nero?"

"Yeah, that miserable soul," Arturo replied.

"Yeah, I've heard from Charlemagne about him. He seems interesting."

"Charlemagne saved my life. I don't know whether I should be grateful about it or not."

"Why?"

Arturo didn't reply.

"You don't have to tell me," Diana replied. "Do you smoke?"

"Why?"

"Because I have smokes and I'm going to smoke," Diana responded, taking out her cigarettes.

Arturo watched as she took out a cigarette and brought it to her lips. She then fetched her lighter but couldn't find it.

"Ah, crap," Diana remarked.

Arturo watched and fetched a lighter from his pocket. He then passed it to Diana.

"If my cousin, Dino, finds out about me smoking, he'd whip me," Arturo remarked. "He emphasizes healthiness – it's a tradition of ours even though half of the family still smokes. It's not that hard to find a carton of cigarettes in the mansion."

Diana blew out her smoke. She passed her cigarettes to Arturo who took one. He then lit it up and the two smoked together.

"You know," Arturo said to Diana in his solemn tone, "I understand your frustration about your mom's death. I feel the same about my own folks."

"You feel guilty about it?

Arturo nodded.

"But didn't Nero kill them? Why is that your fault? You couldn't have saved them."

Arturo didn't say anything more. He finished his cigarette and then stood up. He looked down to Diana.

"I don't believe that your mother's death wasn't your fault, Diana," Arturo said to her. "You can't blame yourself for the actions of other people. You can only own up to your own direct errors."

Diana watched him as she put out her cigarette. He took a step back.

"Thanks for the smoke," Arturo remarked, "but I have to head to class. You should go too."

"Yeah…" Diana replied, standing up. "Wait."

Arturo stopped and looked to her. Diana caught up to him and the two walked back to the main building together. They then entered the quiet halls and came to the junction.

"I've got science," Diana said to him.

"I have math," Arturo replied, looking at her. "I'll see you."

"Yeah," Diana replied, moving towards the stairs.

"Wait," Arturo remarked to her, turning. "You know, you were telling me about how you were Catholic – I know you might not believe in that stuff, neither do I, but when it comes to coming together as a community, church is nice. My whole family is Catholic, being Italian of course, so I was wondering if you'd like to come to church with me and my family this Sunday. We don't go to St. Allan, but to San Francesco di Paola in Calabrese Plains – for Latin Mass. I can have a car brought for you, and we can go together."

"That sounds really nice actually," Diana replied to him. "Yeah."

"Great," Arturo replied, smiling to her. "I'll see you then."

Diana smiled back at him and then walked upstairs. She gave a light laugh as she came to the top steps and then went to class.

•

At the end of the school day, Diana returned to her locker and fetched some books. She then closed her locker and went downstairs to leave school and wait for Charlemagne. She looked around the various cars that were parked around and the kids outside. She couldn't see Charlemagne, so she decided to walk forward to the sidewalk. There, she looked up and down before starting to walk down.

Diana saw a man in a cheap yellow plaid suit stand next to his expensive red sedan. The man had a toothy grin on his face and hands in his pocket. His suit matched his hat over his head. Diana walked by him only for him to side-step and put himself in Diana's way.

"Excuse me, miss. Are you Diana Cambridge?" the man asked.

"Who's asking?" Diana aggressively replied. "What do you want, creep?"

The man laughed and then presented a business card.

"The name's Barney," the man greeted in a coarse accent. "Barney Cohen, and I own the Allabrese Equestrian Center. How'd you do?"

Diana took the business card and didn't respond.

"I missed you and Charlemagne at the track on Friday, but that didn't stop me from catching you and that wild horse whilst crossing the bridge. It was only afterwards that I realized who you were, and well, I want to offer you the opportunity of a lifetime."

"My horse is not for sale," Diana replied.

The man laughed.

"No, nothing like that," Barney said. "Nothing like that. No, I was going to offer you to compete in the upcoming Nattau Derby later this month. A horse like yours would kill on the track… figuratively, of course."

"My horse isn't a racer," Diana replied to him.

"Oh, but he is," Barney remarked. "To race is within a horse's blood, especially yours. That horse of yours is an outlaw. It's intractable and it's untrainable. The horse has a spirit that no human can tame, so I thought until I saw you with it. Yes, with you at his side, the two of you could set new records and dominate! Of course, both of you would need to do a lot of training before the first race, but that can be paid and arranged."

"The two of us?"

"Yeah, kid," Barney replied. "The two of you. Nobody else can ride that horse but you. And look at you, you're the perfect size to be a jockey. How much do you weigh?"

"About a hundred pounds," Diana answered.

"Perfect! And your height is borderline, but okay…. I could get a uniform specially made as soon as went for a fitting."

"I'm not a horse trainer," Diana said to him. "How are we supposed to train?"

"I'll pay for it and arrange for my best trainer to help you out. His name is Sean Cavanagh," Barney remarked, taking out a metal case and searching for a business card. "Here, he's the best instructor and coach this side of the Nattau River. He used to be a jockey when he was young, but then he grew and that was that. You and that horse of yours will be in good hands though."

"Zephyr," Diana corrected. "My horse's name is Zephyr."

"Zephyr, that's a good name… a little confusing. I would have personally gone with Hurricane, but that's just me. Listen, kid. You and Zephyr will be racing champions by the end of the season. I guarantee it!"

Diana looked at him and looked to the side.

"You're a criminal though," Diana said, looking back at him. "I heard it from Charles. You stole the equestrian center from his dad – you're known to cheat. I don't want any part of that."

"Bah, kid. I don't cheat. His old man lost the center fair and square – the man was a gambler and the thing with gambling is that you'll always lose eventually."

"And you 'guarantee' we'll win? How? By giving my horse steroids?" Diana questioned.

"No, no!" Barney replied. "I won't even go near that horse. I'm not mad! If I were to go near your horse, I'd get my teeth kicked in!"

"Okay, so what do you get out of this? I assume you want to increase your profits, but what else?"

"Oh, I get the satisfaction of knowing that I made a little girl's dream come true," Barney remarked.

"It's not my dream to be a jockey, so what do you really get?"

"Fine, if I can sell you to the people, I could double my profit this season in ticket revenue. If you sign up with me, you'll have to sign a contract that authorizes me to collect all revenue in relation to your merchandising, public signings, all that sort of crap. I'll be your manager and sponsor, but of course (hopefully) you'll have other sponsors and I'll have the full right to collect those profits. You'll just have to sign a contract, collect the signature of your guardian, and bing bang, we're in business."

"Charlemagne would never agree to that sort of thing," Diana replied. "And what do I get out of this? What does my horse get out of this?"

"Well, your horse gets to run as it was born to do, and you.. I don't know... What do you want? Money?"

"I want to get paid," Diana asserted. "In cash. I also want cigarettes delivered to me on occasion."

"What a perfect combination. You were born for this. I tell you," Barney remarked. "You've got a deal then. I'll pay you a fair stipend by the week and get you some cigarettes, and in exchange, you race for me. Does that sound good?"

Cohen offered his hand for them to shake on it. Diana thought for a moment. She frowned and then looked at the man with a serious face.

"Kid? Come on, kid," Barney insisted. "Don't leave me hanging."

"Fine," Diana replied, shaking his hand. "I'm in."

Act 3, Scene 2

Charlemagne arrived at the steps of the Cabernet Industries head office in downtown Allabrese. He entered the main entrance, which was decorated with black marble walls and floor tiles. He had a briefcase in hand and his phone in the other as he went to the elevator.

The elevator ascended to the third floor where Charlemagne walked out and put his phone away. He passed the reception desk and walked down a corridor towards his office at the end of the hallway. He entered through the glass door and stopped as he saw all the people inside.

"Mr. Cabernet, I'm sorry, but I didn't know what else to do," Charlemagne's secretary said from behind his desk.

Charlemagne saw about half a dozen people in black suits, two of which were sitting down and had stood up. The others stood behind them and they were all turned to Charlemagne.

"That's quite alright, my dear," Charlemagne replied, taking off his grey hat and putting it atop of the coat rack.

Charlemagne then took off his coat.

"Who are these people?" Charlemagne questioned, walking around the side of the room, keeping cool and calm.

"They said they were friends," Charlemagne's secretary replied. "I didn't believe them."

"Quite alright, my dear," Charlemagne replied. "You can return to your desk. I'll be fine."

The eyes of the men in their suits followed him. Charlemagne's eyes went over to the door of his office as his secretary left. Charlemagne then sat down and the two in front of him, an older and a younger man, sat down.

"I thought I asked Dino to stop sending his men here," Charlemagne remarked, putting his hands together.

"Dino?" the older man asked in his Londoner accent. "Mr. Cabernet, I believe you are confused. We know nobody of that name nor are we associated with anyone of that name. We come from Harlech and I simply request a moment of your time."

Charlemagne looked at the older man before nodding and relaxing his hands at the side of his desk. He was dressed in a black suit and black tie. His grey hair was combed back. Next to him was a younger man in a similar suit, but with short and neat black hair. He also had grey eyes.

"I know who you are," Charlemagne remarked, wagging a finger at him. "You've aged, but then again, so have I. You're Oswald Montgomery, the so-called 'Leader' of the Harlech Syndicate."

"I have no relations to any crime syndicate," Montgomery replied. "It's good to be recognized even at this age, but I prefer to be known for my work in developing the leading security company in the country: Paladin Group."

"Yes, but we don't get to choose how we are remembered. Everybody remembers you for instance for your charisma and desire to take Harlech into a 'New Age'," Charlemagne remarked. "Of course, then you had that scandal and such affairs in the eighties…"

"Lies and slander, Mr. Cabernet," Montgomery replied.

"What is it that you want?" Charlemagne questioned. "My company does not deal with criminals nor do we intend on joining your union or contract from your security company."

"I'm sure of that, Mr. Cabernet, but our interest goes beyond business. Please, let us just talk."

"Very well," Charlemagne replied, leaning back in his seat.

"Mr. Cabernet, allow me to introduce to you my associate here," Montgomery raised a palm for his colleague seated next to him. "His name is William George Cambridge although he prefers to go by 'Willis.'"

"Very good to meet you," Charlemagne responded, nodding to Mr. Cambridge. "So, how can I help you?"

"Well, Mr. Cabernet, we have a particular interest in your adopted-daughter," Montgomery remarked.

"Why? What has she done?"

"Oh, nothing that could endanger herself – it's nothing of that sort," Montgomery replied. "You see, our interest in Ms. Diana is that—"

"She's my daughter," Willis replied in a thick American accent. "I would appreciate it if she were returned to me."

"What?" Charlemagne questioned, looking at Willis and focusing his eyes on him. "Of course, you're William Cambridge…?"

"Yes, and as it seems, it appears that my daughter has been mistakenly put under your care," Willis said.

"I don't understand," Charlemagne stuttered. "How is this possible? I did my research and learned that both of her parents had died in separate incidents. You were murdered at the hands of these people!"

"Well, let's not believe the lies of the media," Montgomery remarked with a smile. "I'm not expert into the death of Mrs. Cambridge, but Mr. Cambridge here has been alive and well. You see, we staged his death so that police could cease their interest in our friend. Willis here was not always the star employee of my organization, so we sought to change that. We invested in him many rigorous hours of training and discipline, and we crushed his laziness and recklessness out of him to make him the model citizen you see before you. He is now a prestigious member of my organization as second-in-command."

"If this man is Diana's father then why was he missing all these years and away from Diana? She was arrested and thrown into foster homes for almost six months before she was brought to me!"

"Well, it took time to whip Mr. Cambridge into shape, but when he did, it was unfortunate that Diana's mother was gone and it was also impossible to find Diana. She was an outlaw and an urban legend – she soon became a thorn in our side and impossible to capture, but there was no reasoning to her. And then, she disappeared and then it was truly impossible to find her until we learned of her existence in your care not too long ago."

"And we're here to bring her back home," Cambridge added.

"Yes, you see, there's another detail that is worth mentioning," Montgomery said. "Over the years, Diana had accumulated a large debt to us over all the damage, stolen goods, and other items she's taken from us."

"How much?" Charlemagne asked.

"Well, let's not dread on exact amounts, but it's in the hundred thousands," Montgomery remarked.

"Well, you're her father," Charlemagne said, looking at Mr. Cambridge with suspicion. "Why don't you pay off your daughter's debt?"

"Mr. Cabernet," Willis replied. "What kind of man would I be if I paid off my own daughter's debt? A man like you should know better!"

"Very well, and do you expect me to simply hand Diana over to you based on this conversation alone?"

"Well, it would be nice, but our intentions are to communicate to you what we want. We want Diana back in Harlech where a promising career with us awaits."

"I want to redeem myself to her as well," Willis added. "For all the years that I was a terrible father, I aim to make up with interest."

"Diana is smarter than you believe her to be. Diana holds greater potential than with your kind," Charlemagne responded, standing up.

"Mr. Cabernet, my business and yours are not so different," Montgomery scolded. "It would be hypocritical to contrast us, especially when your corporation can achieve much more than what mine could."

"And we wouldn't want to bring the police into this," Mr. Cambridge replied, "or the press and the courts."

"Diana was brought to me under the legal authorities of Her Majesty's government," Charlemagne responded, "so by no means will I give her up so easily."

"I want my daughter back," Willis argued, standing up.

"That will be for her to decide!" Charlemagne shouted.

"I'm her father!"

"I'm her guardian."

"Enough!" Montgomery yelled. "Willis, that's enough."

Mr. Montgomery stood up and offered a hand to Charlemagne. They shook as they gave each other serious faces.

"Mr. Cabernet, we came here to talk like civilized people," Montgomery said. "We signaled our intentions and have accomplished our task here. If you'll mind, we will be leaving now. Have a good morning, Mr. Cabernet."

Mr. Montgomery left, taking his coat from the coat rack before walking out with his crew. Charlemagne watched them off before sitting down. He took a deep breath and turned around to look outside.

"What the hell was that?" Huxley asked from behind.

Charlemagne turned back around to look at him.

"Who were those people, Charles?" Huxley remarked.

"Our old friends from Harlech," Charlemagne replied. "Mr. Montgomery and the elite of the Harlech Syndicate."

Charlemagne explained to Huxley what had just happened.

"Oh, God," Huxley replied, standing up from his chair. "Do you believe them?"

"Of course not," Charlemagne responded. "I'm sure they're interested in Diana because she's irritated them and see potential in her to join their ranks. Or perhaps they're simply here to bribe me."

"Well, whatever their motivation is," Huxley said, buttoning his blazer. "I'm sure it was something worth travelling all the way here from Harlech. After all, if one of my kids were in the hands of a complete stranger, I would leave the instant I knew to go find them."

"Yes, I would too," Charlemagne replied, sighing.

"If they're to return, should I have security called?" Huxley asked.

"No," Charlemagne responded. "Not yet."

Act 3, Scene 3

A red luxury sedan pulled along the side of the narrow road in front of the Cabernet Mansion. Diana then stepped out in her pink dress and grabbed her backpack. She was wearing a pink dress with a bow tied around her waist.

"Alright, kid," Barney boasted from the wheel. "Your uniform will be ready for tomorrow when I pick you up from school. You did good for your first week, but we have another week ahead of us before the race on the fifteenth. Don't sweat it – the two of you are coming along well."

"Alright," Diana replied as she stood in the light rain. "Anything else?"

"Nope," Barney replied, "just enjoy your first pay. You earned that money!"

"Yeah, thanks," Diana replied, closing the door.

The car drove off and then made a wide U-turn ahead before racing off. Diana waited until it was gone before opening the gates and going up the steps to the front entrance of the mansion. She took her keys out from her backpack and began to open the door to escape the cold. Once the door was unlocked, she entered and jumped as she saw Charlemagne walking out of the living room.

"Jesus…" she whispered.

"Diana!" Charlemagne greeted. "How was your day? Did everything go alright?"

"Yeah, it went swell," Diana replied, giving a fake smile. "After the service, I went to Arturo's home and spent the rest of the day there."

"Excellent," Charlemagne replied. "Listen, can you come to my study? I have to discuss something with you."

Diana froze and didn't reply. Charlemagne walked over to the corridor before the library and then motioned his hand for her to follow him.

"Come on," Charlemagne said, "you're not in trouble."

Diana followed and entered the library with him. The mansion library had a healthy amount of books in its shelves since last season. The two of them walked past and entered Charlemagne's study. They walked to his desk were Diana sat down in front of it while Charlemagne sat behind. The ticking of the grandfather clock behind them was all that could be heard as Charlemagne paused for a moment. Diana looked to the side and saw a cabinet with Charlemagne's ghost hunting uniform on a mannequin and various tools next to it. The main weapon was hung up by fishing wire.

"I'll be brief," Charlemagne said, looking to Diana. "I wanted to inquire about your father, if I could."

"My dad? Psh, he was biggest scum that ever walked this Earth," Diana replied. "He was a crazed alcoholic, misogynist, and bastard. I didn't want anything to do with him, and to be frank, I'm glad he's dead."

"When did he die?"

"When I was eight," Diana replied. "He didn't show up at the apartment for about a week, and then we learned from the cops that he had been found dead. My mom took it hard, but I didn't care. I was a little relieved and the only remorse I felt was for my mother because she loved him."

"Right, and since you grew up in Harlech, can I assume you're knowledgeable about the city?"

"Yeah," Diana replied. "Why?"

"Are you familiar with the Harlech Syndicate?"

"Yeah, of course I am."

"Well, I came to work last Friday and sat down to be met with a group of shady figures from Harlech. They were led by Mr. Oswald Montgomery, the owner of Paladin Group, his private security company."

"Really?" Diana questioned with a smile "They're here?"

"Yes," Charlemagne replied, "and Mr. Montgomery was with a man who they claimed to be your father, William 'Willis' Cambridge."

"Impossible," Diana reacted. "He's dead."

"Yes, I know, Diana," Charlemagne replied, "which is why I must ask if you know for one-hundred percent certainty that your father is dead. Did you go to his funeral? Was his body there or did they cremate it?"

"What? No, we never picked up the body or held a funeral," Diana responded. "He was cremated and my mom spread his ashes somewhere."

"How could my dad be alive?" Diana questioned. "Why would he be with the Harlech Syndicate to pick me up and why would they be with him?"

"I'm not sure, but there's more," Charlemagne went on.

Charlemagne explained the meeting in detail from the fact that Willis was trained and disciplined, faked his death, and was now back to claim his daughter.

"He wants to see you again," Charlemagne finished. "He's passionate about having you return to him."

"He can go to hell!" Diana shouted, standing up. "I never want to see him again! He's garbage! He doesn't deserve me anymore than he deserved my mom! I don't want anything to do with him! I can't believe the syndicate would betray me like this…!"

"Please, calm down, Diana," Charlemagne replied. "I'm not forcing you back to him, but I wanted to leave the option up to you and only you."

"No! I'd have to be crazy to want to see him again! I hate him more than anything in the world! He hasn't changed – he'll never change! He'll never love me! It's too late for him – tell him that! Tell him that it's too late for him to win me back!"

"I'll be sure to pass that on if I ever see him again," Charlemagne responded. "Unfortunately, he seemed adamant about it and they may go to the courts."

"Good, I'd like to see them try! I'll tell the court all the fascinating stories I have about the countless times he put me in endangering situations."

"Very good," Charlemagne replied, clearing his throat. "Now, since I have you here, I wanted to also talk to you about getting involved in the community. I took the liberty of picking up this brochure at the community center and thought I'd hand it to you to see about some sort of afterschool activity you might be interested in."

"What?" Diana questioned in a calmer tone. "Why?"

"Because community involvement is important," Charlemagne replied. "Although you may be hesitant at the moment, you'll see that one of these things might be right for you to choose from.

"Look at this for example," Charlemagne said, pointing. "They have lifeguard training starting this March. You could look into that and make yourself a career that pays well."

"Yeah… maybe," Diana replied, looking at the overly happy girl on the brochure.

"Anyways, I'll let you take this and think about it. I'll be happy with whatever you choose," Charlemagne responded.

"Right…" Diana replied, lifting a smile. "Thanks, Charlemagne. I'll think about it and bring any paperwork that needs signing straight to you so I can start as soon as possible."

"That's the spirit," Charlemagne smiled. "I'm glad you think this is a good idea."

Diana continued to smile as she stood up and left his study. Charlemagne took a deep breath.

"Well, that went better than expected," Charlemagne said to himself.

Diana rushed through the library and made it back to the main entrance where he crossed Tristan who had just come downstairs. Tristan watched her go upstairs before he went into the library and then walked up to the door of Charlemagne's study. He then knocked on the door and waited.

"Come in," Charlemagne shouted.

Tristan opened the door and stepped inside.

"Ah, what is it, my dear boy?" Charlemagne asked with a smile.

"Nothing much," Tristan replied, walking over and sitting in the chair in front of his desk. "Did you talk to Diana just now?"

"Yes, I had something private to talk to her," Charlemagne responded. "It's nothing too important."

"Was it about her hanging out with Arturo Medici?" Tristan questioned.

"Oh, no," Charlemagne responded. "Diana is free to make whatever friends she wants to… even if their family holds a bad reputation."

"Then, was it about how weird she's been behaving?"

"No, not that either," Charlemagne replied, "but I do know what you're talking about. What can I help *you* with though, Tristan?"

"Well, I was actually thinking about you, Charles. I wanted to know more about you."

"What about me?"

"Well, to be specific, I wanted to know about your personal, romantic life," Tristan explained.

"Oh, well, that's quite an ask. I don't suppose I've ever really been asked that before," Charlemagne replied, leaning back in his seat. "Are you having girl troubles?"

"Kind of," Tristan replied, looking to the side.

'Well, how could I help you then?"

"I just want to hear about the kind of romances you've had first," Tristan responded. "Have you had many? Were they short? Long?"

Charlemagne laughed.

"Well, I've had the short infatuations and the long romances," Charlemagne reminisced. "I was almost married once upon a time too."

"What stopped you?"

"Well, I made the unfortunate decision to travel to Switzerland to support a Cabernet research team led by some of our doctors. They were experimenting with fusion technology, which was very advanced for that day and age. I believe the year was 2000, and this was an unfortunate time to fly out to Switzerland as it was on the night of our four-year anniversary – January 17. I stood her up at the bottom of the Eiffel Tower and it was the last time we talked because she wouldn't answer her phone. I'm sure she hates me with every fiber of her body, but it's okay because it's what I deserve."

"Ouch, that's terrible," Tristan responded.

"Yes, poor Manon," Charlemagne sighed. "She'd be better off with anybody but me for that display of carelessness. Over the last years, I've come to regret it more than I did at the time.

I haven't dated anyone since then, especially since a part of me still aches for her."

"Wow," Tristan remarked, looking at a picture of Charlemagne, Diana and Tristan on the bookcase. "Who was your first love?"

"Oh, the first girl I fancied was a schoolmate at my preschool in England. I believe her name was Rachel..." Charlemagne thought aloud. "And then my second girlfriend was during the summer after I returned from England. You see, I attended school in Harlech, but I returned to Allabrese during the summers, and during one summer I fell in love with your principal, Sabrina Dawson. It was merely a summer romance and didn't last, especially since Cole stole her from me and they haven't separated since then... During university, I met Judith and we dated for about a year but we separated and stayed friends when we realized that we had different visions. And then, during a convention in Germany after I became chairman of Cabernet Industries, I met with the daughter of my mentor, Mr. Dumas, who was a childhood friend – Manon Dumas, and she became our archeological consultant for the Cabernet Expedition team. She worked with us whilst we were doing some research around the ancient and medieval world, but we didn't fall for each other until after our expedition in the Central/Eastern Europe. It was only those months after the expedition team broke up that we actually went on dates and even lived together. We had an apartment in Paris, and it was the quietest two years of my life."

Charlemagne looked back to Tristan as he straightened up.

"Wow," Tristan replied. "I'm impressed... up to the part where you stood her up."

"Why are you asking all this?"

Tristan sighed.

"Because, there's a girl in my grade who I like, but I don't know if she likes me back," Tristan explained.

"Oh, it's like that then," Charlemagne responded, bringing a hand to his chin. "How does this girl act around you?"

"Well, she's been ignoring me even though we used to talk a lot. I don't know if that's because she really likes me, or because she really dislikes me. I was okay with us being friends, but then after we had this intense moment during last summer, I started to have feelings for her, but I've been repressing them and it was okay – I thought I could move on and stay as friends. But then Halloween happened, we bonded and had another intense moment which caused these feelings to burn inside me, and then there was another incident not too long ago where we were naked – well, I was naked, but now I can't stop thinking about her because I'm crazy for her and I'm tearing myself apart, because I'm not sure if I'm annoying her and need to distance myself or if distancing myself might be too much because I think she's interested in some other guy now... and she's so damn beautiful and I just want to love her, but I can't and it's making me mad!"

"Alright, calm down," Charlemagne reasoned, hushing him. "That was a lot to take in."

Charlemagne took a deep breath and then looked over to Tristan.

"Well, it appears this relationship with her has become complicated to say the least," Charlemagne stated. "If you feel this strongly about her, why don't you confess it to her and let her know?"

"What if she rejects me?" Tristan replied. "I can't handle that because I have to see her almost every single day... at least until I graduate. I also don't want to bother her – I'm pretty sure she has issues that don't concern me, and I don't want to be a bother."

"Right," Charlemagne replied, stroking his chin. "It would be bothersome to present yourself at a moment where she might not be ready or have the time. Well, in this case, find out if you annoy her and be there for her. What might be best if you're simply there for her to listen to her problems and if it seems like you're annoying her, ask and distance yourself, but be sure not to suffocate her at the same time."

"Okay..." Tristan said, sighing and standing up.

"Is that all?" Charlemagne questioned.

"Yes," Tristan replied, "thank you."

"No problem," Charlemagne responded, typing into his computer as Tristan left. "Oh, and Tristan?"

Tristan turned to him.

"I have a favor to ask from you," Charlemagne stated. "I know you're bothered over your woman issues, but given the circumstances of Diana's behavior, I need you to keep an eye on her for me. You're her friend and she trusts you. I don't want her to be alone – that's another reason why I'm okay with her talking to Arturo, it's because she needs friends to rely on."

"Right..." Tristan replied, nodding. "I'll do that."

"Thank you, my boy, and best of luck with your own problems."

Act 3, Scene 4

"I look… just great," Diana sarcastically jibed.

Diana looked at herself in her uniform. She wore tight white pants and black riding boots that went to her shins. She also wore a red jersey over her torso, which matched her black helmet in-hand. She had tied her dark-brown hair into a bun so that her helmet would fit. A knock on her dressing room door caused her to turn around and put on her helmet.

"Hey, kid," Barney said, entering the room. "We're on in about ten. Are you ready?"

"Yeah, I guess," Diana replied, walking over to him.

The two left the dressing room and walked down a long corridor to reach the stall where Zephyr was being kept. The stall was very large and spacious, and it also had a heater. The horse went to the gate as he saw Diana.

"Hey there," Diana said in a soft voice, brushing his forehead.

"Alright, get your horse ready," Barney said, taking a step back. "That horse has a temper… we couldn't even get the staff to put on the saddle and bridle."

"Yeah, he prefers if I do it," Diana replied, opening the gate and fetching his saddle. "Come on, Zephyr. It's showtime."

Diana slid the bridle onto Zephyr's head and secured the holster in his mouth before securing the saddle. She then led him out of his stall and down the corridor. Barney led them out of the stables and onto the racetrack outside. It was dark outside, but the lights of the arena made it seem like day.

Zephyr and Diana walked out onto the dirt and could hear the light murmuring of the audience in the stands. She could also hear the announcer on the P.A. system, making banter with his co-host. The two of them walked down and followed the other horses to the starting gates. The crowd wasn't that big, but there were TV crews all around the sidelines and journalists with their notebooks and cameras.

Diana looked uneasy as she walked towards the starting gates. A lot of cameras had flashed at her and she was only halfway to the gates. She decided to look forward and behind at the other jockeys. She had deduced that she was the youngest and one of the few females. Diana also looked around at the entire racecourse, seeing the extent of the stands with the private viewing gallery above the place where she and Tristan were seated. She could also see how the barn stretched out from the main complex at a slight angle. At the opposite-side of the racetrack there was a metal fence at the banks of the river.

Finally, she reached the gates where she mounted Zephyr and led him into his gate. The workers closed the gates behind her and confined them to their stall. The other horses neighed and thrashed around. Diana was calm in contrast as was Zephyr. Diana felt sweat under her gloves. She held the reins tight and tried to breath slowly.

The announcer mumbled in the background as the other horses screamed. Diana closed her eyes to focus on her breathing. She then opened them and focused in front of her.

The sound of a fire alarm shook violently and the gates opened. Zephyr jolted out.

"And it's go, go, go!" the announcer called out. "We've got Thunder leading himself forward followed by Diamond Dozen and Cocoa Butter. Immediately behind them we've got Win It and Foxy Lady coming along down!"

The rest of the horses followed as they rode the first meters in close proximity. They all nudged to the inner perimeter of the racetrack. A man in a yellow jersey and another in a magenta jersey took the lead while Diana stayed in the middle of the group.

Diana looked ahead as the leading jockeys whipped their horses violently, causing them to accelerate. Diana held her whip but refused to use it. She instead held it in her left hand whilst keeping focused in front. The horses galloped forward and with the yellow jockey and magenta jockey gaining a lead from the others.

"Uh oh," the announcer shouted, "looks like we've got Zephyr and Blue Moon falling behind! Thunder is in a tight battle with Cocoa Butter for first place alongside last year's champion, Win It, around the back."

Zephyr lagged behind and was soon last in the stream.

"Come on, buddy," Diana said as they galloped along. "Just like we practiced – speed up!"

"Oh no, it looks like Zephyr can't keep up, but we have Cocoa Butter showing it to Thunder and Win It as he steals first place from them as they come around!"

Zephyr took deep breaths as he tried to keep up, but it was no use as the others simply sped up faster than him. There was almost a five meter gap between them and the horse in second-last place.

Diana held the whip in her hand and looked to it.

"Come on, Zephyr, you've got to try harder!" Diana urged. "Please."

The duo continued to lag behind.

"Please, Zephyr, we can do this! Come on, buddy," Diana pleaded. "I believe in you."

Zephyr looked to the horses in front of him and began to rush harder to start a sharp acceleration forward. The jockey in a light blue silk jersey looked behind him to notice Diana and Zephyr speeding up at an alarming rate. He took his whip and began to slap the rear of his own horse, Blue Moon, in hopes but was soon passed.

"Win It steals second place from Thunder, but Cocoa Butter takes a sharp lead from the others. Ooh! Thunder takes second-place again in this tight race for second-place!"

Diana looked ahead of her and saw the rears of the horses trudging along and blocking him from advancing without pushing through. She looked for an entrance, but then decided to steer Zephyr to the side to pass them. Zephyr zoomed by as they came around the third corner and then the final corner.

"Oh, it is looking close folks!" the announcer hyped. "We've got Cocoa Butter falling back with Thunder against him. Win It has stolen third-place, and now we have this fourth competitor battling Win It for first – Diamond Dozen!"

"Heeyah," Diana light said, pushing Zephyr faster as they came to the final four hundred meters.

Zephyr continued to race past the horses, making his approach behind Thunder and Cocoa Butter at the three-hundred meter mark.

"A little more speed, buddy," Diana motivated, tossing the whip. "Come on!"

Zephyr breathed furiously as it stomped his hooves in the dirt and pushed forward to come behind Thunder and Win It.

"Two hundred meters, we have Thunder a little ahead of Cocoa Butter and Win It going for first place and Diamond Dozen in second place. Remembers, folks, the top three will be moving on from this qualification round to participate in the derby on behalf of Allabrese, but it looks like it'll be a tight one tonight!"

"Come on, let's do it!" Diana whispered to Zephyr.

Zephyr continued to push himself harder and harder. He started to pass Thunder and then approached Cocoa Butter.

"Cocoa Butter is moving ahead, but – whoa! Look at Zephyr speed along at the one-hundred and fifty meter mark. He's not stopping, folks! Look at him go!"

Diana held the rears tightly as he felt the speed and wind brush against his face. Zephyr pushed himself towards Win It who had fallen behind Diamond Dozen.

"I can't believe this! Zephyr is hitting it home and he's not stopping! That is some killer speed!"

"Yeah, let's go, Zephyr!" Diana cheered.

"Zephyr overtakes Win It for second-place. Oh my – he's going for first at the last fifty meters. Is he – oh, he does it! Zephyr steals the show! Ladies and gentlemen, Zephyr and his rider Diana Cambridge have stolen this race from our seasoned vets. I repeat, the dynamic duo, Zephyr and Diana, who are making their debut this season have stolen the show from last year's champion, Win It. Diamond Dozen comes in second place and Win It in third. Wow, I don't believe this folks... was your heart racing too or just mine? What a race!"

The crowd cheered for them as they slowed down past the finish line. Diana led Zephyr to turn him around and face the cameras as she smiled over her victory. The applause roared at them and gave them a standing ovation. Diana then led the horse over to receive their prize, a ribbon, a bouquet of flowers for Diana, and a garland of flowers for Zephyr to eat. She gave a light smile as they had their picture taken before they went off to return to the stables.

Barney clapped at the entrance of the stables.

"Amazing, kid!" Barney cheered. "You had me worried, but you did it! I haven't seen a comeback like that in years! If you can keep this up for the rest of the season, we'll have that trophy in no time!"

"Thanks," Diana replied, smiling as they walked. "Give my thanks to Sean as well."

"Or you can thank me now," a man replied at the entrance to the stables corridor.

The man spoke in an Irish accent. He had dark grey hair over his head and wore a blue suit. He was in his fifties and had scruff around his jaw. Diana hopped off Zephyr and hugged her coach.

"Thanks," Diana said, "your training paid off."

"Well, it was fine work you put in, but I'm afraid it only gets harder from here on out. The others won't be pleased by this outcome, and horses from other cities will be studying you seriously. I'm afraid that's the cost of winning first place. We have a lot of work ahead of us."

"Sure thing," Diana replied, leading Zephyr back to his stall.

"Alright, it's good to plan for the future, but we have to celebrate this occasion," Barney remarked. "I mean, winning your first race is something you *have* to celebrate!"

"Okay," Diana laughed, "let me just drop off and say goodbye to Zephyr."

Diana returned Zephyr to his stall and hugged him. She then let go and walked out to return to her dressing room. By the time she got there, Barney was already drinking champagne.

At about midnight, Diana took a taxi back to the mansion with her flowers in hand. She walked up the steps of the mansion and entered with the flowers in-hand. She then went to her room, crossing Tristan's room which was open. Tristan raised his head from his desk and then stood up to stop under his door frame. He saw Diana enter her room with a bouquet of flowers and then close the door behind her. He frowned, closed the door behind him and returned to his desk.

"Oh no…" Tristan remarked, "they're getting serious."

Act 4, Scene 1

Diana raced at the Allabrese Equestrian Center again having raced at Grand Prairie, Red Deer, and Edmonton already.

"Oh, here it is folks," the announcer shouted. "We've got the deviant duo: Diana Cambridge and her horse, Zephyr, coming along with Drop Down close behind and then followed by Pathfinder and Bell Bell.

"Come on, let's go," Diana whispered to Zephyr.

Zephyr pushed himself.

"Bell Bell overtakes Pathfinder, but Drop Down can't keep up – oh, it's going to be close!"

Diana and Zephyr stormed across the finish line for the fourth time in her career and began to decelerate as he turned to the cheering crowd and absorbed their spirit as she smiled back at them.

"And there we have it again, folks," the announcer remarked. "Zephyr comes in first with Drop Down in second, Bell Bell in third, and Pathfinder in forth. What an amazing race... and to think that this is the debut of Diana and Zephyr with the two starting their careers less than a month ago... last month."

The crowds, which were more dense than last month, cheered for Diana. She continued to grin before going over to receive her fourth ribbon in the season, winning the Allabrese Stake. In total, there was about four times the amount of people than in March.

"You know, Ms. Cambridge is truly astonishing us," the announcer proclaimed. "She's defeated all of the eighteen qualifying horses in the province three times now, not to mention their victory at the qualification round for the Nattau Derby."

Diana received her ribbon and flowers. Zephyr received another garland to eat. The two then took their picture with Sean and Barney before parting to go to the stables.

"Well, folks, that concludes the Allabrese Stake tonight. It was an alarming minute and a half, but was worth the wait, I'm sure. We look forward to hearing from our homegrown troops, Thunder and Zephyr, who are in the lead to compete in the national round next week. In the meantime, goodnight and God Bless, everybody."

"You're doing amazing, kid," Barney cheered as they walked down the track. "The crowds love the two of you, and that's been great for tonight. We haven't had a show sell out in years!"

"Another win gives us another five points towards being able to represent Alberta in the nationals," Sean said, taking off his hat. "We already have fifteen points from our earlier victories, so at twenty, no matter what happens, we'll be in the nationals… provided we don't come in last place."

"But that won't happen," Barney replied, "because this little miracle and this little miracle," he said, pointing at Diana and Zephyr, "are going to win the Calgary Stake."

Diana and Zephyr came around to the barn before going down the corridor of stalls to reach Zephyr's.

"Come on, let's get Zephyr inside and resting," Sean said, leading Diana down the corridor as she continued to ride atop of Zephyr.

"I'll catch you two in the dressing room," Barney remarked. "I've got to head to my office and do some… counting. Kid, tremendous work tonight! I haven't seen a horse win this many stakes in a row since Beansprout back in the late-eighties!"

Sean shook his head and then looked up to Diana.

"I'm proud of the two of you," Sean remarked. "Watch your head," he warned as they got to the stable and he opened the gate. "Are you coming in or getting off?"

"I'm going to stay with Zephyr for a moment before I go home if that's okay," Diana replied.

"Sure, just duck your head then," Sean said. "Zephyr deserves a nice and soothing rest after this win. I'm thinking of having him take the day off tomorrow to rest before we get back to training for next week's race in Edmonton."

"Yeah, I'm sure Zeph would appreciate that," Diana replied.

Diana tilted her head to avoid the beam as she rode Zephyr into his stall. He then hopped off and began to brush him. Sean removed the garland from his neck and set it somewhere so he could eat it later. Diana finished brushing her horse before she removed the saddle and bridle.

"Rest easy," Sean said in a soothing voice. "Both of you."

"Thanks, Sean," Diana replied, smiling to him. "Thanks for everything."

Sean left the two of them and walked off. She continued to brush him until she put both hands on the sides of his face to look at him through his pitch-black eyes.

"I'm so proud of you, sweetie," Diana said. "You have no idea how happy you make me with all we're doing. Each race is better than the last, and I know we're going to win this thing. I hope you're as excited for it as I am."

Zephyr didn't respond and simply looked back as he listened to Diana's soothing voice.

"I hate that I have to leave you and go home. I'm so happy here, but then I go home and I'm depressed again. It makes me not want to skip out on training tomorrow, because I know I'll be upset – would you be upset too? Every day, I look forward to getting to climb onto your back and gallop around with you,"

Diana said, closing her eyes as she hugged him. "The chance to ride around sets me free – it's like being in Harlech again, except I'm not. I'm here. The bright side is that all this anger within me is pushing me – your anger is pushing you. We're going to do this, because the fire burns within us!"

Diana let go of her horse and smiled at him.

"You know, I had a rough day today too, and I didn't think it would get better even though I knew we had a race today, but I proved myself wrong. I owe you a lot, Zeph. I hope that all of this is enough to repay you. If not, I'll be in your debt. Thank you."

Diana hugged Zephyr again. The horse lowered his head to accept the embrace of his sole trusted friend before raising it up as she let go.

"I'll come around tomorrow with some treats," Diana said. "If we don't have to train, I'll at least take you for a ride. Goodnight until then."

Diana kissed Zephyr on the cheek and collected her flowers and ribbon on a table nearby before going to his gate, opening it and stepping out. Zephyr walked towards her but stopped as he saw the gate close. She locked the gate and then rushed down the corridor to get to her dressing room. She entered and placed the flowers on a table in the middle of the room. She then took off her helmet and looked at herself in the mirror. She untied her bun and allowed her hair to be free. Diana then fixed her latest ribbon on the wall before taking a deep breath. She then went to grab her clothes to shower, change clothes, and then get ready to leave.

By the time she was stepping out of her dressing room, the corridors were quiet. She walked down, said goodnight to Zephyr once more, and then went to the entrance of the equestrian center. She sat down and couldn't see Barney anywhere. She looked around for him before opening the door to step outside where she saw two luxurious black sedans along the curb of the sidewalk in front of the sports center.

Each car had tinted windows and gaudy ornaments at the hoods of the cars. The rear-passenger seat door of the second vehicle opened, and a man in a fine black suit stepped out and removed his fedora to reveal his thick black hair.

"Diana," the man greeted in his Scottish accent.

Diana looked back at him with surprise. She then began to smile at him.

"Do you remember me?" the man smiled.

"How could I not?" Diana questioned, rushing over to him and hugging him. "Scot!"

The two embraced for a moment before they parted.

"I thought that was you when I was at the airport last January. How've you been?"

Diana heard some voices from within the car. She leaned over and looked inside.

"Hey, you're here too!" Diana remarked to some more members.

Diana retracted her head and then looked to Scot.

"Wait a minute," Diana said, dropping her smile. "I have a bone to pick with you people! Why is my father alive?"

"Ack, your father's not alive," Scot replied. "Come on, we'll explain everything."

"What?"

"We tried to butter up your grandpa, but he wasn't buying it," a man inside the car explained in his Liverpool accent.

"Nah, I'm your father," Scot joked, putting on an American accent. "Don't you recognized me? It's me, Willis!"

"Very funny," Diana replied, shaking her head. "I wish you were my dad."

"Hey, I wish you were my daughter," Scot replied in his regular accent, smiling. "Come on, we'll take you back to that mansion of yours. The pig of a man known as your manager isn't coming. We paid him off so we could have this moment to ourselves."

"Sure," Diana replied, taking off her satchel to step inside.

Diana entered the car and sat in the middle. She looked to a man on her left, sitting across from her. He was looking out the window before she entered. He was old and had slicked back hair.

"Oswald…" Diana remarked, bringing her hand up, "it's an honor."

"Please, Ms. Cambridge," Montgomery replied, taking her hand with both hands. "The pleasure is mine to get to meet such a special girl as yourself."

Montgomery let go and looked to Scot as he entered the car and closed the door behind him.

"Well, knowing that my father is still dead has brought a great relief off my chest," Diana confessed. "Do you have any more good news?"

"Plenty," Oswald remarked, "but first, how about a drink?"

"Oh, I don't drink," Diana replied.

"Oh, that's right!" Oswald reacted, tapping his cane into the floor of the car. "How foolish of me. Perhaps a soda then?"

"Yes, please," Diana said.

"Give the kid a soda," the man with the Liverpool accent said.

Diana was handed a soda can to open.

"Albert, please take us to the Cabernet Manor at once," Oswald ordered.

'Yes, my Leader," Albert replied from the front of the car.

"So, what have you been up to, my dear?" Oswald asked. "We haven't heard from you in years – it was noticeable because we received a significant drop in shoplifting incidents."

"Well, I got kidnapped by the Feds and brought here," Diana remarked with a sad tone. "Now I live in the middle of nowhere in the Cabernet house."

"Well, moving from one of the poorest neighborhoods in Harlech to one of the most expensive properties in the country is certainly something," Oswald said. "I knew you would find yourself in such a situation, but I never imagined it being like this."

"How's Charlemagne treating you?" Scot questioned. "Is he too tough? Should I have another word with him?"

"He's fine, Scot. Calm down," Diana remarked to him. "He's a good guy and a good guardian."

"You like it here then?" Scot asked.

"Well, it's alright," Diana confessed. "The home is a bit too big, but it has a nice library. I also have a brother – although, I don't like calling him that and neither does he. His name is Tristan. He's nice and I like him, but I don't think he likes me and to be honest, I don't like being around him right now because of it."

"Oh, you have yourself a crush then," Scot remarked, smiling.

Diana blushed.

"I do miss the city," Diana also confessed. "You know, I miss running along the streets and running away from cops. I also miss my mom, but that's something that can't change."

"I'm sorry about your mother, dear," Oswald said in a sad tone. "Scarlett was a wonderful woman. It's a shame your father corrupted her as he did."

"Thanks…" Diana replied. "So, what brings you people here? Is there a convention or something?"

"Well, that's just it," Scot answered. "We've come for you."

"You see," Oswald explained, "ever since Damian saw you at the airport, he's been trying to track you down so that we could come and see you. You know, we've always kept a close eye on you. We've watched you grow from a petty thief to an accomplished mugger, and we were impressed with you throughout. You grew up on the streets and were hardened by them like a man is hardened by his time in the wilderness. You were diligent in surviving, and we recognize you to be superior than the average human."

"So, what?" Diana questioned.

"So, we're offering you a position in our organization, Diana," Scot said. "We went and talked with that loon, Charlemagne, to give you up, but he refused. We can't go to courts since I'm not actually your dad either."

"So, we're reaching out to you," Oswald added. "We're here to offer you this chance to return home and be the person you were born to be."

"Are you serious?"

"Dead serious," Scot confirmed.

"I don't know…" Diana replied, dropping her head.

"What are you future intentions, Diana?" Oswald questioned. "Another couple of years of public education and indoctrination? A fancy degree at some Marxist institution? Come with us, and you can start early and build yourself up. You have the potential and promise, and it's time to act on it. One day, you might come to run this organization after I pass on."

"Well, not after me too," Scot added with a smile.

"You salty seal," Oswald scolded him with a smile. "I'll have Diana run the syndicate faster than I have you do it. Anyways, what do you say?"

"What do you think?" Scot asked. "An orphan like you will have her mansion and fancy cars in her own city of Harlech. You deserve this lifestyle, but the problem here is that you haven't earned it by being adopted by some loon. What is earned is more worthwhile, wouldn't you say?"

"Yeah…" Diana replied, "but I don't think I can just leave what I have here. I mean, I'm a horse racer, I have friends here, and I have… family."

"Family?" Oswald questioned with a confused look. "Right, well, I didn't expect you to make a decision because I knew the type of lass you are, Ms. Cambridge. I expected this from you because you're a clever one. What I've proposed is a major decision and like all major decisions, they need and take time to decide upon."

The car slowed down and came to a halt. Oswald produced a business card from his blazer and gave it to Diana. It was a business card for the local restaurant.

"When you've made your choice, come to us here," Oswald said to her. "We'll be in town until the end of the month. Until then, we'll be running operations from this restaurant, The Broiled Buffalo."

"Think carefully about your future," Scot warned Diana, "your entire life ahead of you depends on it."

"Right," Diana replied, "thanks, Scot."

Scot opened the door for Diana. He stepped out and offered her a hand. Diana took it and came out.

"Until then," Scot said to her, "please, take care."

"Thanks," Diana replied, hugging him again. "You too."

The two parted and Scot stepped back into the car. The two cars then drove off and disappeared down the road. Diana sighed as she watched them off.

Diana looked at the picture of a buffalo with a steam cloud over its head. She then turned it and looked at what was written. There was a local phone number and a name, 'Jerome.'

Act 4, Scene 2

Tristan got dressed after drying himself and his red-blonde hair. He was in the changeroom after gym at the end of the school day and after gym class. He then tied his shoes and left the changeroom to walk up the stairs that went to the gym. From there, he walked across the gym floor to the stage and exited via the stage exit.

Meanwhile, Diana showered in the girl's changeroom across from the boy's room. Diana stood motionless in her stall with cold water beating down against her long blackish hair to splatter strands along the crown of her head. She silently stood there with soap in-hand. She put the soap away and turned off the tap. She then exited and grabbed her towel to dry herself.

Diana pulled her black shirt over her skin before dragging her grey jeans up and putting on her denim jacket. She sat down and pulled up some socks and then her shoes, and then she put her gym strip into her satchel before exiting the changeroom. Diana walked upstairs to the top of the staircase and entered the gym.

"Boo!" a voice said from behind her.

Diana turned and smiled as she saw Arturo above and against the railings of the bleachers. He climbed over the railing and jumped down to join her.

"Congratulations at the stake yesterday," Arturo said with a smile. "I wish I was there to see you win it."

"Sorry, I should have invited you," Diana regretted. "Not only because it was local and a sold out show, but also because I would have loved if you were there."

"Hey, it's alright," Arturo replied. "Do you want to go have a smoke behind the bleachers before you go for practice?"

"Oh, I'm not going to practice today, but I might head down to the equestrian center to say 'Hi' to my horse," Diana explained as she led him towards the gym exit. "We're taking the day off to rest before the semi-final next Sunday. It's in Calgary."

"Wow, that's pretty far away," Arturo replied.

"And you're welcome to come to this one if you want," Diana invited. "Please."

"I would love to," Arturo smiled.

Diana and Arturo exited the gym and came to the field behind the school. They started to walk towards the bleachers. The warm spring sun patted down against them as they made their way across and towards the bleachers.

"I have to thank you," Arturo said. "I took your advice and got feedback about my songs from Mrs. Rivers, and she loved them. She said they were good."

"I told you she'd think positively of them," Diana replied.

"Yeah," Arturo responded with a shy smile.

The two continued to chat as they made their way across the field and behind the bleachers. Once behind, Arturo offered Diana a cigarette and the two started to smoke together.

"I have a lot of schoolwork to catch up on," Diana confessed. "I'm barely holding my grades together."

"I thought I told you to stay balanced," Arturo replied. "You might not know what you want to do, but that doesn't mean you won't know in the future."

"I've never really thought about my future because I've always had to think about the present," Diana remarked. "I don't even know what I'd want to do – I mean, I want to be a mom one day, but what more?"

"We're still young," Arturo replied. "You have lots of time left."

"Yeah, but when it comes to you boys, you have you entire lives already set out," Diana remarked. "I mean, you guys know that you have to get jobs eventually and make a life for yourselves, but it comes so naturally to you. Tristan wants to go into medicine. Peter wants to go into medicine too. You want to go into business because you'll be leading your family business eventually."

"Nobody says that you have to get a job though," Arturo remarked. "It's mainstream society that wants you to get a job, especially for a woman, so that you can feel 'empowered.'"

"How can I feel empowered when I'm slaving away for some corporation? I'd rather give myself to my own children," Diana replied, looking to the side before looking back to Arturo. "You know, you remind me of someone now, which is funny because I just saw him yesterday."

"Who?"

"An old friend from Harlech visited me yesterday after my race. He used to protect me when I lived on the streets."

"Do you like him?"

Diana laughed.

"I do like him, but I don't *like* him, although I did have a crush on him when I was younger. I see him more as a father figure than anything else though. He's older than me by about thirty years."

"Oh, it's like that then," Arturo replied with a sarcastic smile.

Diana dropped her cigarette and squashed it with her foot. She then stepped to face Arturo. She looked at him and his blue eyes and clean face. His black hair was long, but not too long. Diana brought a hand up to touch his smooth cheek. He turned his face to blow smoke away from her before looking back at her.

"I *like* you," Diana confessed, lowering her hand to his waist.

"I like you too," Arturo replied, looking down, "but Diana, there's something you should know before we kiss."

"What?" Diana reacted. "Please don't tell me you're gay."

"No," Arturo replied, smiling at her, "I'm not. I'm attracted to you, but I also respect you a lot and don't want to make it seem that us being friends is anything more than it is – that I'm leading you on because I really do like talking to you and it's not about romance with me. I like being your friend and my intention at the start was to be your friend, but I also do feel like I want more with you now because you're beautiful, smart and funny. My point is, I don't want to hurt you, especially since I don't know if I'm going to be staying in Allabrese."

"Wait, what?" Diana reacted again. "What do you mean?"

"You know how I've been talking about wanting to go into business? Well, Dino says that since my grades aren't the best, my chances of getting into a good university are slim. He's suggesting that I enroll in one of the elite private schools and wants to send me to an expensive prep school in Harlech for grade eleven. It's a boarding school."

"Oh…" Diana responded, letting go of his waist, "so, you'd be in Harlech."

"It's not just about me getting into a good university," Arturo added. "Dino is also afraid that me being in Allabrese isn't good for me, especially at this school because he thinks I'm being bullied."

"Right. Well, if you think this is the best for your future, go for it," Diana replied, looking back at him.

"Well, I wanted to ask you for sure if I should do it because I'm starting to really like you, Diana," Arturo said to her, "and I don't want us to have any hurt feelings by expanding how we feel about each other anymore than it is right now."

"Yeah…" Diana responded, shrugging, "I don't know, Arturo. This isn't my decision to make – it's your future. I don't know if I can make that decision for you."

"You have to," Arturo insisted, "because I can't make it on my own. I'm torn between the two."

Diana and Arturo looked to the side and through the cracks of the bleachers as they heard a whistle being blown.

"Crap, field hockey practice," Diana remarked, taking Arturo's hand, "come on, let's walk and talk."

The two came out from behind the bleachers and started to walk together back to the school.

"Listen," Diana said to him as they walked, "I like you a lot too, and I'm not saying this because of what you've told me, but I'm divided. I'm going to tell you this because you deserve to know."

The two stopped behind the school near the patio tables and beside a door inside.

"My heart's divided between you and another boy right now," Diana confessed. "Ever since something happened last year, I've felt terrible around him and can't stand being near him because he ignores me and it hurts me not being able to love him. I know he's not gay because I've seen him interested in other woman, so that makes me believe that he doesn't see me anything more than a friend – I'm glad I know that's not the case with you."

"Who is he?" Arturo inquired. "Is it Justin? Or Alex? It isn't Jock?"

"What?" Diana questioned. "When have you seen me ever talk to those boys?"

Arturo went silent.

"It's Tristan then," Arturo replied. "Of course it would be him."

Diana put her hand over Arturo's mouth.

"Nobody can know about this. Understand?"

"Yeah," Arturo replied, "but why are you telling me this?"

"Because I can't procure a relationship with you until I'm at peace with these feelings that have been eating inside of me," Diana replied. "I want to be with you, and I want you to love me, kiss me, and hold me – these are words I've never said to anyone, but I live with Tristan and he's someone I'll be likely seeing for the next two years."

"I don't understand," Arturo said. "What's so special about him?"

Diana sighed. She then began to explain to Arturo how she met Tristan, the first adventure they had in the mine, the second adventure they had during Halloween, and the third adventure in Russia where she had to save his life by keeping him warm with her body. By the end of the Russia story, Diana was crying.

"Hey," Arturo said, hugging her.

"I- I exposed my body for him," Diana remarked. "I stripped myself to my underwear, and... he could have died that night. He could have died like my mother died, and it would have been my fault because I didn't know any better. You have no idea how eerie it is to be next to someone, unable to feel their heart, but only able to feel the slight breath seeping out of their mouth – their dying breath as that little bit of life slowly fades away and you're left with the doubt over whether they're alive or not."

Diana continued to cry.

"Things have never been the same since that night," Diana said. "He tries to pretend like it never happened, but it did happen. I nearly lost him, and it pains me to think about it and see him not even be affected by it. He almost shows no gratitude whatsoever for what I did, and it bothers me! It bothers me how he shows no care in the world! It peeves me! He behaves the same way with his parent's death! Why?! Why can't he show a little emotion?"

Diana pushed away from Arturo.

"And that's something I've liked with you," Diana said to him. "You haven't resisted to show me any emotion. You're honest with me. You tell me what's wrong and I've seen you cry too."

Arturo didn't reply as he looked at Diana.

"I'm sorry about this," Arturo finally said. "In fairness though, it took a lot for me to open up to you. It's just that way with men, I guess. It's not like we're sociopaths. We do have emotions, but we save them for ourselves because they're precious to us... and we only like to share them with those we deem trustworthy. Not just anyone, but our special someone – a girl we trust and who would understand. That's' why men aren't usually emotional with other men, I think."

"I guess I'm not special to Tristan," Diana replied, calming down. "This isn't fair to you."

"It's not fair that I might have to move to Harlech," Arturo added. "It's a precarious situation, and I'm okay with it. I'm glad you told me."

Arturo continued to hug Diana before they separated as soon as she calmed down.

"Come on, I'll give you a ride to the equestrian center so you can say 'Hi' to that horse of yours," Arturo said, letting go. "I'm sure he'll cheer you up."

Diana laughed.

"Yeah, he would."

Act 4, Scene 3

"Our reports from the last fiscal year showed us destined to have a steady marginal increase, but recent reports from the last quarter show a sharp decline in profits," an older man explained.

The man, Martin Bowman, was an older board member at least ten years older than Charlemagne. He had thick dark grey hair that was slicked back. He also had fair skin and an oval face.

"The biggest concerns, however," Mr. Bowman continued, "is the drop in the value of our shares. The prices have dropped considerably since the start of the latest quarter and show no sign of recovery. We need to take action before this destroys us."

"What can be done then?" Zimmerman questioned from the table. "The attack against Mr. Cabernet last December startled investors more than the rumors that the company was going to be liquidated. A numerous amount of Mr. Cabernet's private schematics were leaked online as a result of these mercenaries stealing his laptop, and some have said to have been found on the black market."

"Profits are shrinking, and all we can do is restore confidence in the public that we are in control," Huxley replied. "Our image is important."

"Perhaps it's time that Cabernet Tech is liquidated once and for all?" Zimmerman suggested. "It's a liability. I mean, that fusion reactor alone took millions to build and failed us."

"We are not liquidating Cabernet Technologies," Charlemagne interrupted in a strict voice. "I founded that division, and I'd rather die than have the labs shutdown."

The board members groaned.

"Please, Charles," Zimmerman pleaded from his side of the table. "Be reasonable. I know you understand that this division is a liability to your company."

"The difference will have to be made up by other divisions until Cabernet Tech can make ends meet," Charlemagne responded. "I will not approve of any liquidation. It's together or none at all."

Charlemagne's phone began to vibrate. He took it out and read the notifications on the screen. He received a text message from an unfamiliar number to him. The area code told him it was from Harlech somewhere. Various additional messages followed the initial text message, causing his phone to vibrate multiple times. Charlemagne unlocked his phone and read the first message. The message contained a link for a local Harlech news network.

Charlemagne tapped the link and watched his screen load the article. The article was titled, 'Fatal shooting in Keswick believed to be targeted.' Charlemagne scrolled past a picture of a random alleyway to read the article in depth. 'William Cambridge, 29, was found dead in an alleyway between Mackenzie and Borden Street in the Keswick district on January 16 of this year. The victim was declared dead on-scene by police and was found with multiple gunshot wounds to the torso. An in-depth investigation by police suggests, however, that organized crime could be a key factor in the cause of death although the spouse of the victim denied that her husband was involved in any wrongdoing.'

Charlemagne closed the article and tapped on the second one, which was titled, 'Chinese Frigate destined for Harlech, sunk in Dalian harbor.' Charlemagne paused for a moment before closing the article and going to the next. The article was titled, 'Overdose deaths reaches one-hundred percent increase in Harlech since 2012.' Charlemagne frowned and opened the next, which said, 'Oswald Montgomery denounces Opioid Crisis amid record death tolls – blames 'Big Pharma.''

The latest article caused Charlemagne to raise an eyebrow. He scrolled down. 'The 77-year old business tycoon has spoken out against the recent opioid deaths despite claims that the Harlech Syndicate are behind the opioid trade. Mr. Montgomery denied any involvement when questioned about his company's roles in enabling drug trafficking. He suggested that his company was working hard to counter illegal drug trafficking, which the legal authorities have neglected and permitted to corrupt the city. The business tycoon also stated that any news source that says otherwise is simply, 'Fake News' and a distraction from 'Big Pharma,' referencing the conspiracy theory that pharmaceutical companies are behind the opioid crisis.'

After the last article, Charlemagne read a message from the anonymous messenger, which said, 'We are not your enemies. There are darker forces in the world, and Diana will need protection and guidance.'

Under this text message were two more articles, the first from a mainstream news source and the other from a less mainstream source. Charlemagne opened the first and read the title of the article, which said, 'Mysterious thief strikes again in Keswick.' The article then continued to say, 'A mysterious thief who has been raiding stores across both Keswick and Bromley on King Island has struck again, causing local businesses to petition the Harlech Police Department to take action. A witness, who would prefer to remain anonymous, came across the thief while shopping at the Kitchener Drug Store on Vanier Avenue last June, described the thief as "young and possibly in her early teens.' The witness specifically mentioned that she thought the thief to be a female, which matches what most other witnesses have reported.'

Charlemagne closed the article and went to the next, which was a PDF research essay titled, 'The Secret Child of King Edward VIII and Wallis Simpson.' The article continued, 'In this essay, a series of secret documents from the CIA and private letters belonging to Ms. Simpson suggest the royal couple birthed a son, which they kept secret from the Allies. According to these documents, Ms. Wallis Simpson gave birth to the boy whilst in Portugal, which the CIA (formerly OSS) was aware of during the war. The couple, of whom were suspected of spying for the Axis, were devastated when the child was taken from them. CIA documents suggest that the child was taken to Canada and placed in a foster home. The documents also provide a series of possible surnames that were to be given to the child – the original first name of the child is currently unknown. Possible surnames include, 'Albany, Buckingham, Cambridge, Cleveland, Stuart, Sutherland, Tudor, Wales, and Wellington,' although it is uncertain which was chosen.'

Charlemagne rolled his eyes and then went back to his text messages. He saw that he had been sent a document. He opened it and scrolled through the various pages to see that it was similar to the last essay, but in depth and signed off by the Paladin Investigations as a detailed report following an investigation. Charlemagne turned off his phone and stood up.

"Charles?" Huxley questioned, looking to him.

"I'm sorry, but I have to step out for a bit," Charlemagne complained. "I believe my back is getting to be a bit stiff. Please, if there's any major decisions that need to be made, go ahead and make them."

Charlemagne left the meeting room and walked down the corridor back to his office. He opened the door and stepped inside. He went to his desk and turned on his computer, and while the computer loaded, he sent the last document sent to him to his own email. The item sent just as Charlemagne's computer woke up. He went to his emails and opened the item on his desktop to read. The report was close to one-hundred pages long, but Charlemagne carefully read through it. During the beginning, he noted an address on a sticky note, '15868 Bennett Street, Unit #12.' He continued to read, taking the entire hour to finish the report before he laid back in his chair and took a deep breath. He then went back to his computer screen to re-read the last paragraph, which stated, 'Our intentions with Ms. Cambridge are to safeguard her from the Chosen and to ensure that she can be raised in a suitable environment and receive the appropriate instruction that she needs for her own survival and prosperity.'

After Charlemagne had finished reading the document, he closed it and turned off his computer. He then looked at the sticky note and picked up his phone.

"Ms. Young," Charlemagne spoke, "please transfer me to Mr. Bond. I need him to fly me to Harlech as soon as possible."

"Certainly, Mr. Cabernet," Ms. Young, Charlemagne's secretary replied.

Charlemagne waited for the line to connect.

"Hello?" a male voice answered.

"Hank, it's me, Charles," Charlemagne replied. "Listen, I need you to come to Allabrese to pick me up and take me back to Harlech. It's important."

"Sure, I can be there in twenty minutes," Hank replied before hanging up.

Charlemagne put his phone down and stood up. He went to grab his coat and hat before stepping out with his briefcase. He walked down the corridor and came to the reception desk. He called for his elevator as he turned to Ms. Young

"Is everything okay, Mr. Cabernet?" she asked.

"Yes, everything is fine, Trude, but I'll be heading out," Charlemagne responded. "Please, enjoy your Friday evening and I'll see you next Monday."

"Goodbye, Mr. Cabernet," Ms. Young replied.

Charlemagne entered the elevator and then had it come down to the lobby. He walked down to the main entrance doors and stepped out to the street. He then walked down the sidewalk, went down an alleyway between the head office lobby and a real estate office to reach the rear parking lot. There, he walked to his car and entered. Charlemagne left his briefcase in the passenger seat, turned on the car, and then pulled out. He drove through downtown Allabrese and then went towards the bridge. He drove over and started to drive northwest towards the airfield. He parked his sedan and then waited.

About ten minutes later, his private jet descended from the skies and landed on the airstrip. Charlemagne got out of his car and walked towards it as the stairs opened for him to enter. He then met Hank Bond at the top and shook his hand.

"Sorry for the late trip," Charlemagne remarked.

"Hey, if it's Harlech, it's no problem," Hank replied, walking into the cockpit with Charlemagne. "What's the important mission?"

"Oh, I just need to visit Keswick and see something," Charlemagne replied. "It's concerning one of my children."

The jet flew from Allabrese to Harlech within ten minutes. The plane touched down gently once it was cleared to land, and Hank then steered it towards a private hangar. From there, Charlemagne exited and entered a car waiting for him.

"Where can I take you, Mr. Cabernet?" the driver asked as Charlemagne entered.

"I need to go to 15868 Bennett Street, please," Charlemagne said.

"Sure thing," the driver replied, tapping into his GPS. "In Keswick? Are you sure?"

"Yes, it's important," Charlemagne insisted.

"Okay, Mr. Cabernet," the driver complied.

The car pulled away from the hangar and drove to a checkpoint before being cleared to join regular traffic out of the area. From the airport, the car drove and merged onto the highway that ran through Cliffe Island, over Durham Bridge, onto Jarsdel Island, and then along the highway until Marke Bridge before coming off near Industrial District. The car exited onto Bailey Drive and drove north from Bromley into Keswick.

From Bailey Drive, they drove right onto E Stuart Street where the traffic was thick. The traffic thinned once they turned right onto Bennett Street and then continued until they passed Mackenzie Street. Finally, the car reached the apartment complex where the cab pulled up along the curb. Charlemagne could see the four-story building from his passenger seat window.

Charlemagne exited the vehicle and walked towards the steps entering the apartment building. He read the names of the tenants of all twelve apartments. At the top of the list, at Unit #12, was surely the name 'Cambridge.' Charlemagne stepped away from the door as an older woman pushed through and left the building. He caught the door before it closed and entered.

The front entrance had cracked terracotta tiles and an exposed brick wall. The entrance was small with just a wooden backless bench against the right wall above the beaten-up mailboxes. There was another door ahead with wooden planks over the cracked windows. Charlemagne pushed against the door before opening it to step into a dark stairwell.

Some loud shouting could be heard from the door on the immediate right, Unit #3. Charlemagne stepped up onto the first step of the stairs, hearing the creak of the step before he made his next. He walked up and came to the second floor, which had a similar appearance to the front entrance. He then made his way up to the third and finally the fourth floor where there was a simple option between four doors at either side.

Charlemagne walked over to Unit #12 and knocked on the door. He waited for someone to respond, but nobody answered. Charlemagne then knocked again before he put his hand onto the brass knob. He tried to turn it, but it didn't' turn. However, as he pulled on the door, it moved. Charlemagne then pushed on the door and it slid open.

The unit had a small corridor, about a yard long, that led forward. On the right there was a wide closet in the wall, and on the left was a kitchen. The floor had scratched dark brown floorboards ahead and into the living room while the kitchen had white-black tiles. Charlemagne walked inside and looked around. On his right, next to the closet, was a large graffiti mural painted on the grey dry walls.

The kitchen was small and only had a circular white table which was on its side due to a missing leg. The counters were cleared of any appliances and there was no refrigerator. The cabinets were missing their doors. The entire area was extremely dirty. The kitchen blended into the living room, which only had a sofa with springs sticking out. Charlemagne walked around the couch and went towards the door on the left of it.

Charlemagne pushed against the bedroom door and entered the spacious room with a single mattress on the floor on his immediate right. A door across from the mattress, on Charlemagne's left, led into a very small bathroom. At the end of the bedroom was an open window with a crow pecking at something on the window sill. The window led onto the fire escape in the alleyway at the right-side from the main face of the building. Charlemagne looked around for another second before he left.

Outside of the apartment, across from Unit #12 was a man sweeping dirt from the floor in front of his unit. Charlemagne closed the door behind him and looked at the man. He had dark white skin that was wrinkled. He also had dark grey hair.

"Excuse me," Charlemagne interrupted the man, "but does anybody live here?"

"Nobody live there now," the man quickly replied in a scratchy accent. "The girl... she gone."

"Do you own this building?"

"I am landlord, yes."

"Do you own this unit here?"

"No," the man replied, "I do not own. Man who used to live there own it."

"William Cambridge?" Charlemagne asked.

"Cambridge, yes," the landlord replied. "He dead. Home belong to wife, but she dead too. It now belong to daughter, but she gone. Unit belong to government until she claim when she nineteen."

"What happened to Mr. Cambridge?" Charlemagne questioned.

"He killed," the man remarked, looking to him with his cold eyes. "He bad man – made mafia mad."

"Are you sure he's dead?"

"Yes," the man replied, "wife scattered ashes from roof."

"I see," Charlemagne responded, nodding. "Thank you."

Charlemagne then left down the stairs and left the building. His phone vibrated as he left the building. He swiped it and read the newest text message sent from the anonymous number. Charlemagne opened the link sent.

The article was from the local Allabrese newspaper, the Allabrese Chronicle, and it was titled, 'Wonder Woman, Diana Cambridge, wins first place at Allabrese Stake, furthering her winning streak."

"Is this some sort of joke?" Charlemagne muttered, scrolling down.

Charlemagne scrolled past a picture of a jockey riding a black horse. The article continued and said, 'Fifteen-year old Diana Cambridge won first place at the Allabrese Stake last Sunday. Her victory was her fourth in a row since her debut at the qualification round last March with her horse, Zephyr.'

"I don't believe this," Charlemagne frowned, turning off his phone. "I won't be fooled by these liars."

Charlemagne walked back towards the car and entered. He slammed the door behind him and laid back.

"Harlech International, please," Charlemagne requested before turning his head to look out the window.

Charlemagne gave a sigh as they drove out. He stayed quiet for the rest of the trip home.

Act 4, Scene 4

Tristan clicked the top of his pen and tossed it onto his math notebook before pushing himself away from his desk. He put his books into his backpack on the ground and then opened the compartment in his desk to retrieve his laptop. Inside this secret compartment were other treasures, including a photo of him and Diana in front of the Neva River with the Winter Palace in the background.

The sound of a footstep approaching caused Tristan to immediately close the compartment and close his door slightly so that it was only cracked open. Diana walked past with her satchel on her back. Tristan stood up and opened his door. He watched Diana enter her room before he closed the door again. He could hear the shower running in the other room and decided to wait before standing up again as soon as it was off. He waited another couple of minutes and started to pace around his room. After ten minutes, he stood up and left his room. He marched down the hallway and stopped in front of Diana's door where he hesitated to knock. Once he did, he held his breath.

Diana opened the door and held a grim look on her face as she looked at him. She was dressed in a sweater and yoga pants. Her hair was tied back and her bed cover was pulled over. The light on her desk was the only light turned on.

"Hi," Tristan greeted, exhaling.

"What do you want?" Diana questioned.

"How was your day?" Tristan asked, giving a nervous smile.

"Busy."

"Where did you go today?"

"Same place as always," Diana replied, rolling her eyes. "The community center doesn't grow feet and move around."

"Right..." Tristan responded, lowering his smile.

"Are we done?"

Tristan didn't respond and Diana didn't wait for an answer. She left her door open as she turned her back and went towards the bathroom.

"Where are you going?" Tristan asked.

"Where do you think I'm going?" Diana questioned.

"Can you blame me for asking?" Tristan replied to her, getting angry.

Diana paused and turned to him with surprise.

"Because it can mean either of two things," Tristan said. "Either you're going in there to use the bathroom, or you're going in there to... to open the window, climb onto the roof, and smoke."

Diana didn't immediately respond.

"And?" she questioned.

"What the hell is wrong with you?!" Tristan shouted. "Why are you acting like this?! I thought you'd be happy with the way things are now, but you're not and it's driving me nuts!"

"I'm fine!"

"No, you're not. We need to talk about this because I can't take it anymore," Tristan replied. "I can't take your negative attitude or your sarcasm anymore!"

Diana took a step back as Tristan finished yelling. Her eyes began to form tears.

"What do you care?" she quietly replied.

"What?" Tristan responded.

"What do you care if I'm this way?!" Diana shouted. "I'm nothing to you. After all we've been through, I'm nothing…"

"What are you talking about?!"

"You don't tell me anything," Diana said, tears gushing down the side of her face and going towards him. "You don't see me as anything, but…"

"But what?"

"A friend. If we even are still friends. And do you know how I know why? It's because you don't open up to me and tell me anything. You want to talk about me, but I want to talk about you because it scares me how you don't emote – it makes me fear you."

Tristan was quiet.

"I have no idea what you're talking about," Tristan calmly replied.

"And that's the problem!" Diana shouted, pushing him back and turning around. "You don't see what the problem is while I'm here hurt, you're ignoring the problem."

"I just came here to talk to you," Tristan replied, stepping forward to her with a frown.

"And that's fine if there wasn't something more serious we needed to talk about," Diana argued, turning back to him. "It would be fine if you didn't try to pretend like what happened in Russia didn't happen."

Tristan didn't respond.

"You know what it is and you won't even say it!"

"Enough of this," Tristan remarked, shaking his head and turning to leave. "We're getting nowhere."

"Don't leave me!" Diana yelled, going to him and pushing him back into the wall at the side of her bedroom door.

"Get off me!" Tristan replied, pushing her away.

"Don't shut me out!" Diana shouted. "Talk to me, please, Tristan! Please, talk to me about what's really bothering you!"

"You're bothering me!" Tristan yelled. "You're bothering me because you've been acting weird since we got home!"

"God!" Diana replied, bringing her hands to her forehead. "You almost died!"

"I know that!" Tristan shouted back.

"And I gave myself to you so you could live," she added in a quieter tone as she cried, bringing her forehead to his chest.

Diana lowered her arms, turned her back to him and walked away from him, into the center of the room. Tristan looked at her with surprise and gave a light frown. He looked apologetically to her as he went to her. He stopped before her.

"I didn't know what to do," Diana said. "You fell in the water, and you were shivering. You weren't replying to me, and I didn't know what I could do. I tried to start a fire, but I couldn't. And then I stripped you from your clothes and put you in bed, but you wouldn't warm up. I thought I was going to lose you, but I had one last idea... I stripped myself and got in bed with you to try and keep you warm."

"Diana..." Tristan replied in a quiet tone, "you told me all of this when I woke up."

"I know," Diana replied, calming down, "but it's the fact that I got myself naked to warm you, and you didn't show even the remotest sign of gratitude towards it."

"I was going to say more, but you told me to be quiet."

"And you never brought it up again," Diana said to him. "What happened, happened, and we never talked about it again even though I almost lost you. And it scared me so much, Tristan."

"I'm sorry, but I had no idea," Tristan responded. "I didn't realize almost losing me scared you so much."

"No," Diana corrected, "losing you scares me."

"Hey," Tristan said, grabbing her hand and turning her around.

Tristan hugged Diana.

"And the fact that you didn't care told me that I didn't mean much to you. It told me that if I was in your position, you wouldn't have been as scared as I was if you were to lose me."

"That's crazy," Tristan replied, separating from her to look at her. "Diana, you mean so much to me. I... I really think so."

"It doesn't feel like it. The way you act tells me otherwise – all you care about is yourself. You talk to me and laugh, but that's it. All that tells me is that you like to talk to me, but nothing more. Nothing serious. All I have to do is look at your indirect expressions," Diana replied. "And they told me that you didn't care."

"I do care. I'm here right now, and I'm... I'm telling you that I care."

Tristan frowned at her.

"But I need to show you that I care – prove it instead of claim it."

Tristan hugged Diana again.

"I'm sorry," Tristan confessed. "I seriously do care about you, because..."

Tristan sighed and separated from her again so that they could look at each other.

"Because all I've been thinking about since I realized that there was something really wrong has been you and you alone. It's been bothering me seeing you like this, because... because I really like you, Diana."

Diana didn't respond.

"You left an impression on me when we first met under those bleachers at school. You had an attitude that I hadn't seen in any girl ever. And then you showed up at Salmar's house wearing that dress. I thought you were the most beautiful girl I had ever seen. I've liked you since the start, Diana. And when you distracted those gangsters, I thought, 'Who is this girl?' because I had no idea who you were to be able to stand up to them. Of course, then we became friends and we started to live together, and it made me so happy to live with the most gorgeous girl I had ever met in my life. You made a fair point about me acting differently at home with you than at school, and then we really started to become better friends, which caused me to like you even more. And then, you told me that story about your scar (which I really did want to hear because it made me see more of you) and the thing is, Diana – the more I see of you, the more I like you. And you saved my life, and I didn't realize it took such an emotional toll on you, but I was grateful. I am grateful about it, but I guess I've been too selfish to say anything…"

"I started to like you after I saw you playing on that field that day we met," Diana confessed. "I just thought you were cute then, and after we met, my interest in you gradually increased until it was at its current level now."

Diana and Tristan looked at each other.

"What now?" Tristan questioned.

"I don't know," Diana replied, hugging Tristan.

Diana turned her head so she could look to the side.

"Almost losing you was too similar to when I was dealing with my mom," Diana said, gaining another tear. "I blame myself that she's dead because I didn't know what to do when it came to overdoses."

"What do you mean?" Tristan questioned.

"After my dad died, we hit financial stress because even though he was an asshole, we did depend on him to bring in some money. My mother couldn't work a steady job, so I had to provide. Around this time, I met this man named Damian Sutherland. Everybody calls him 'Scot' because of his Scottish accent. I stole from him. I stole his wallet and used the cash in there to feed us for a week. Little did I know that he was part of the Harlech Syndicate, so one day he caught me and we had a talk. He said I reminded him of my dad. I took that as an insult not realizing that he was talking about certain facial characteristics – in general, he thought I looked more like my mom. Still, I took what he said as an insult and he agreed to let me be if he could get his wallet back since it had sentimental value. In return, he gave me a gun, which I used even though it was empty. It worked as a prop to shoplift with, and so I turned to a life of crime at only ten-years old.

Anyways, this was my life for about two years until I was finally caught. I stole from people, brought the money home to my mom, and that was my day. One day, the shopkeeper kept me around long enough for the cops to show up. I had to bolt it and escape, which I did, but in the process I lost the money. I came home not only late but emptied handed. When I got home, I found my mom choking in her own vomit. I turned her to her side to clear her airway, but I couldn't resuscitate her. I called an ambulance, but when they showed up, it was too late. I didn't realize there was more I could have done to save her. I could have done a lot more."

"Like what?" Tristan questioned.

"I could have had Naloxone around," Diana replied. "I could have trained myself in first aid to properly handle her by putting her in the correct position or knowing CPR."

"CPR would have done nothing," Tristan said to her. "She was poisoned."

"I could have given her Naloxone."

"Diana…" Tristan said, separating from her so they can look at each other, "you're not going to like hearing this, but your mom was responsible for her decisions. You're responsible for yours. You can't blame yourself for her actions. She chose to do drugs even though she had a kid around. Her death is not your fault. If her addiction was bad, it wasn't even her fault."

"I could have saved her," Diana replied with a weak voice.

"But you didn't, and you can go on blaming yourself for her death the same way you could have blamed yourself for my death had I died, but it wouldn't have been your fault. All you can do is learn from this, I suppose, so that you can intervene, but that is the good that comes out of a bad situation. It's what being smart is about – learning from mistakes."

The two went quiet as Tristan went back to hugging Diana.

"I miss her," Diana whispered. "Do you miss your parents?"

"Every day," Tristan replied, pausing for a moment. "You have no idea of the pain."

"No, I don't," Diana responded, pushing Tristan away for a moment.

Diana brought a hand to Tristan's cheek. He looked sad.

"Ever since we started living together, I haven't seen you act emotional once," Diana said. "You bottle up your emotions inside you and that's it."

"It's not like I don't release my emotions," Tristan replied, moving Diana's hand so that they were simply holding each other's hands.

"How? When?"

"At night. For almost every night since they've died, I've cried at night…" Tristan confessed, eyes watering "because it still bothers me. I lost both my parents little more than a year ago, but I do miss them, Diana… I really miss them…"

The two hugged again.

"It's not fair," Tristan whispered to her.

"I know."

The two continued to hug until Tristan opened his eyes and pushed her back gently. He fixed her hair and held his hands around her cheeks.

"No girl should ever have to go through what you've been though, Diana."

"No child should have to suffer what we have felt."

"But this is how life is and how it will always be," Tristan said to her. "I hate knowing that you've been though all this, but I don't regret knowing. It's disturbing that this was your life before, so please tell me that you don't seriously miss all that?"

"It's preferable than being here, with you and your bottled emotion," Diana replied. "All this has torn me open and caused me to suffer because I wasn't sure if you really like me the way I liked you. You weren't giving me a reason to believe that you liked me."

"I didn't want to spoil how it was in case you didn't like me. I like being your friend, Diana, and if I had to stay your friend to avoid rolling the dice on the chance that you didn't like me, then I was willing to accept that because I didn't want to stop being your friend."

"But I love you, you jerk."

Tristan went quiet as Diana's eyes widened.

"I love you…" she said again, hugging him. "You're all I have left. Everybody else is gone and nobody wants me."

"I want you," Tristan replied, tightening his embrace. "I love you too, Diana, but you don't have to take my word for it. Please, tell me if my actions say differently, because I'm just a man. We're all we have left."

"I almost lost you that night."

"But you didn't lose me."

"It was too similar."

"You're not going to lose me, Diana. I love you, and I don't want to ever be apart from you."

"What guarantee do I have?" Diana replied, parting from him.

"You just have to trust me," Tristan responded, looking at her. "The same way you trusted me when we navigated those mountains."

"But you'll be able to find other things in life," Diana insisted. "You're not like me. You're a suburban rich kid with the brain to make a life of your own. You can become a doctor, buy a house for yourself, and live a normal life without me. Why do you need me?"

"I don't need you. I want you," Tristan said. "It's callous, but you don't need me either. We're capable of living our lives separate, but we want each other and there's nothing wrong with that. I can't give you a guarantee. You just need to have faith."

Diana didn't reply.

"You're everything to me," Tristan said, kissing her on the forehead. "And I love you, Diana. I love you so much, and it was driving me mad not being able to say it."

Diana gave a light laugh before looking up to Tristan's green eyes. He showed a light and warm smile to her.

"I love you too," Diana replied as Tristan dropped his forehead to brush against hers.

Tristan's smile widened. The two looked at each other for another minute before they kissed, bringing their salted lips to each other before parting after another minute. They continued to kiss for another five minutes until they separated themselves.

Tristan wiped Diana's cheeks as they looked at each other.

"What kind of people were they?" Diana asked Tristan. "Your parents?"

"My parents? They were honest people. You already know that my dad was a cop and that my mom was a nurse. Between their line of work, they were busy people and hardly got to see each other. In fact, I doubt I've ever seen them really be intimate with each other or express their love, but I know they loved each other."

Diana nodded, looked to the side and then back at Tristan.

"I want to be honest with you, Tristan," Diana remarked in a quiet tone. "You know that horse I found. Do you want to know why it's not in the stalls anymore?"

"Why?"

"On the Monday back to school, I was offered a chance to race with the horse and that's what I've been doing. I'm a jockey. I haven't been going to the community center for lifeguard training. I've been going to the equestrian center for training."

"Wait, really?"

"Yes," Diana replied, "and on Sundays, I race in the Nattau Derby. I've won four races since I started last month."

"That's amazing!" Tristan responded. "Wait, I thought you were going to Mass on Sundays with Arturo. Aren't you dating him?"

"No," Diana replied," I have been going to Mass with him, but afterwards, his family drives me to the equestrian center. I don't spend that much time with him, and we're not dating."

"But, you come back to this place with flowers…"

"The flowers are given to me when I win," Diana replied, smiling at him. "You didn't think I was dating Arturo, did you?"

"Yeah, I kind of did," Tristan laughed.

"You can't tell Charlemagne about this," Diana remarked. "The guy that Charlemagne's dad lost the equestrian center to is my manager, and Charlemagne would flip out if he knew I was working with him."

"Okay," Tristan replied, "your secret is safe with me."

Tristan leaned in to kiss Diana again. Diana held her hand at Tristan's chest. The two immediately parted as they heard the sound of footsteps outside.

"It's Charles," Diana warned, pushing Tristan back. "Hide."

Tristan rushed into the bathroom and left the door ajar. He stayed close to listen as he heard the door knock but closed it for good measure before looking around and then going to the shower. Diana walked over to her bedroom door, fixed her hair and then wiped any wetness on her face before opening the door.

"Ah, good, you're still awake," Charlemagne said.

"Yeah," Diana replied. "What's up?"

"Oh, I just wanted to make sure you're in and all is good," Charlemagne responded, stepping back. "Have a goodnight!"

"Goodnight!" Diana remarked with a smile.

Diana closed the door behind him and then gave a sigh of relief. She then walked over to the bathroom door as she heard the shower running. Her smile faded as she turned her back. She then walked over to her mirror and looked at herself. Tristan washed himself in a fast pace, turning off the water and then grabbing his towel to dry himself. He then walked over to brush his teeth before going back to his room to fetch his sweatpants.

Meanwhile, Diana had stepped away from the mirror and gone to her bed. She entered it and turned off the light. Tristan returned to the door left ajar and opened it. He looked into the dark room and saw that Diana had gone to bed. He hesitated and decided to close the door instead before stepping back and going to his own cold bed to sleep alone.

Act 5, Scene 1

"Welcome, welcome," the Calgary P.A. announcer cheered. "Welcome one and all to the fifty-fifth annual Calgary Stakes. We have a swift team of horses making their way to the gates now, and one grand winner who's going to surely take home one of the two spots for the finals in Allabrese. Tonight, we have the rookie jockey Diana Cambridge and her horse, Zephyr, who are at the lead with twenty points to their name. It's up to the other horses to push forward and snag second place, because at the finale, all these points won't matter and it'll be open season to win the championship cup."

Diana held a sunken look on her face as she rode with Zephyr. Barney and Sean were at either side, walking with her as they made their way to the gates. The Calgary Equestrian Center was larger than the Allabrese Equestrian Center. It held more seats and a larger crowd. Cameras flashed from the darkened crowd. The entire racecourse was lit by lights against the orange evening sky. Diana's hands were trembling and she was looking around.

"You're going to make history today, kid, if you come in first place again," Sean said to Diana as they arrived at the cage.

"You don't have to come in first though," Barney warned with a nervous tone. "You can come in second or third as well, and we'll still be happy. There's no pressure. Heck, even fourth would be okay, but what's important is that you secure your place for the finale."

"Got it," Diana simply replied, entering the cage as the gates shut behind her and Zephyr.

"Best of luck, kid," Sean remarked before he walked off with Barney.

The workers of the racecourse began to lead themselves onto the sides of the gates while Diana took deep breaths. She gently rubbed Zephyr's neck as they waited.

"I haven't talked to him since that night," Diana quietly said to Zephyr. "I missed him on Saturday morning because he had lacrosse practice, and I missed him this morning because I had to go to Mass with Arturo before coming here. Did he mean what he said? Does he really care about me?"

The other horses in the gates neighed. Diana looked around as she stopped rubbing Zephyr's neck.

"Come on," Diana complained, "what's taking so long?"

Suddenly, the bell rang, causing Diana to quickly get in position and rush out with Zephyr.

"Oh, and it's go!" the announcer bellowed. "They're off!"

Zephyr and Diana made a strong push forward, accelerating at an alarming speed and leaving the other horses in the dust. Zephyr galloped forward fiercely. His hooves clambered into the dirt as he sped along to escape the others behind him. The wind flew into Diana's face and she clenched her teeth and held the reins at the side of Zephyr's head with tight fists.

"Zephyr and Diana have immediately taken first place," the announced proclaimed. "Bell Bell lacks behind by about fifty feet. Drop Down and Pathfinder are immediately behind them. Thunder is also lacking behind in fifth. It looks like this race might already be determined."

Zephyr continued to make a fierce barrage forward as the two of them made their first turn on the circuit and along the second length.

"Bell Bell overtook Drop Down again, but not before Pathfinder takes Drop Down as well. I must admit, I'm seeing some slight improvement in Bell Bell's ability. Thunder is still struggling with Crystal Warrior in sixth on his tail. Yes, we have you in our scopes, Crystal Warrior, we haven't forgotten about you. Zephyr is still in first place as they come to the half-way mark."

Diana took staggered breaths as they approached the third turn on the circuit. She let out a sigh and loosened her grip. She held a sad frown on her face and closed her eyes. She then opened them and her ears twitched as she her the brambling of the announcer. She turned her neck to look behind her as she saw two horses directly at her rear.

"Bell Bell and Drop Down have just passed Zephyr! Bell Bell and Drop Down have just passed Zephyr! I don't believe it! Ladies and gentlemen, at the final kilometer, what turn could be happening here?!"

Diana flinched as the two horses raced past her. She steadied her focus and looked at them with a stunned face.

"Come on, Zeph, let's ruin them!" Diana shouted, tightening her grip again.

Zephyr attempted to push forward, but instead of pushing forward they were suddenly pushed back by the two horses behind them in fourth and fifth place racing by.

"Wow!" the announcer shouted. "Pathfinder and Thunder have just stormed past Zephyr as well. What is going on?!"

Diana and Zephyr were taken back by the sudden appearance of these horses. They slowed down and were overtaken by a white horse.

"There goes Crystal Warrior as well!" the announcer remarked.

The horse pushed past Zephyr and almost caused Diana to lose control and fall over. Zephyr marched to the side and out of the way as an entire stampede of horses overtook them. The duo practically stopped a couple of feet from the finish line as their entire competition overtook them and left them behind in last place.

The crowd was silent. The announcer was silent. Diana stopped with Zephyr at the final meters and looked around. She then pushed Zephyr to trot across the finish line before she rushed him to get out of the public eye.

"I don't believe this, folks," the announcer finally said. "What a turn of events..."

"Kid," Barney shouted to her from the entrance of the barn, "what the hell happened?"

Diana escaped into the barn and went past him. She also rushed past Sean and Arturo who were with Barney.

"Kid!" Barney yelled again.

"Drop Down and Bell Bell are tied for first place with a photo finish. We will have to take a moment to determine which of the two beat who in a moment. Either way, Pathfinder takes third place with Thunder in fourth. All horses had an incredible performance during this competition and we've seen some amazing things all around. We're not quite sure where Zephyr and her owner have disappeared to, but I'm sure they're beat up over this loss."

Diana returned to the stable they were renting for the evening. She entered and hopped off Zephyr, hugging him as she let go and cried.

"I'm sorry," she said. "I didn't mean to let you down."

Diana continued to hug Zephyr.

"I just... I was angry at first, but then... then I started to feel bad about being angry and started to feel sad. It's my fault that Tristan didn't know any better, and it's my fault that I haven't talked to him since Friday night."

Diana continued to cry as she hugged Zephyr. She soon calmed down, wiped the tears from her face, but continued to hug her horse.

"What the hell's the matter with you?!" Barney questioned from behind.

"Quiet!" Sean remarked to him.

"First half, you're blitzing by, and then the next half, you decide that you're trotting through a park!" Barney shouted.

"Barnett, that's enough!" Sean said in a stern voice. "A loss was inevitable and there is no blame here. We should have seen this coming, no less on the semi-final race. We've been pushing them both too hard."

"Not hard enough!" Barney complained.

Diana turned around and saw the three of them, Barney, Sean and Arturo. Arturo was quiet.

"Stop," Sean warned Barney.

"Yeah, why should I waste anymore breath with this loser," Barney replied. "This is the Allabrese Stakes loss of 97' all over again. This kid is finished."

"We had twenty points," Sean reminded them. "We can still breakthrough this."

Diana let go of Zephyr and turned to face them.

"We're going to get disqualified."

"No, there's still a chance," Sean encouraged. "Drop Down and Bell Bell both came down to the wire. Each of them only had sixteen points. First place wins you five points, but second place wins you four points."

"We didn't get any points though," Diana replied.

"We still have twenty, but it doesn't matter which of them comes in first or second, because only one of them will surpass us while the other will tie with us. From there, it'll go to the derby committee for them to decide based on the nature and performance of each horse, which should go to us because of our first-place streak."

"Yeah, because the committee will look bright on a horse that just went from hero to zero," Barney remarked, leaving. "If you need me, I'll be in my car."

Sean looked at him and then took off his hat. He ran his hand through his hair before putting it back on. The other horses began to march down the corridor and to their own stalls. Arturo entered their stall and went to stand next to Diana.

"Attention, folks," the P.A. announcer said. "We have reviewed camera footage and determined the final standings. In a remarkable turn tonight, both Drop Down and Bell Bell came to a photo finish, which has now shown that they have truly tied for the first place. Pathfinder retains her third place standing as well as the other horses."

Diana looked over to the TV monitor in their stall. It showed the standings with Drop Down and Bell Bell tied for first place and there being no second place. She glared at the TV and then brought her hands to her face.

"We lost," Diana said.

Arturo put a hand on Diana's back. She removed her hands from her face and then looked back at the TV. The screen had switched to show the net standings. Diana was in third place with twenty points. Drop Down and Bell Bell was ahead of her with twenty-one points respectively. Pathfinder was in fourth place at sixteen points, which included the three points received from today.

Diana cringed as if she had heard a bad joke. She trembled and was quiet.

"I'm so sorry, lass," Sean said to her.

The stall was quiet for a couple of minutes until Sean sighed.

"I'll go and get my truck around. There's no point in sticking around for nothing," Sean remarked, fetching his coat.

Diana looked at Arturo. He had an apologetic look. She looked away from him and over to the TV screen. The monitor displayed the net provincial standings still, but at the end of each contender there was text that said, 'Tentative D.S.'

Sean left the kids behind as they remained in the pen. She looked back over to Arturo.

"I'm sorry this had to happen on the day you were able to come along," Diana said to him. "I... I'm really mad at myself over this."

"Hey, it's okay," Arturo replied. "I got to see you race, and it was better than I hoped, even if you lost."

"It's probably for the best," Diana sighed. "It was nice while it lasted though."

"Attention ladies and gentlemen," the announcer said over the P.A. "According to the derby committee, the standings for the last race have been put on hold pending a drug screening due to the nature of the last event. Please bear with us during these moments."

"Drugs?" Diana questioned. "I didn't even think about the other horses being doped."

"Do you think they were?"

"I'm not sure," Diana replied.

The two waited in the pen until they saw Sean return.

"Did you hear?" Diana said to him.

"What?"

"They're doing a drug test on the horses," Diana replied. "They said that the committee requested this."

"Bloody hell," Sean responded. "Who would be daft enough to try and get away with doping their horse?"

The three of them waited in their stall until a group of people wearing coats that displayed the logo of the Nattau Cup appeared. Sean stepped forward and talked to them.

"We need to examine your horse," an older man with glasses stated. "Failure to comply will result in an immediate disqualification under the rules of the Nattau Derby. Do you understand?"

"Yes, we'll comply," Sean replied.

"We will need to examine your horse as well as produce a blood sample and a urine sample," the leader of the group said.

Diana stayed close to Zephyr as one of the veterinarians walked to the front of Zephyr. He gave an aggressive neigh towards him and backed up.

"Hey, take it easy," Diana warned. "They just want to look at you."

"What the hell is wrong with this horse," the veterinarian questioned.

"He had a rough upbringing," Diana unironically replied.

"Can you control him so I can look at him?" the veterinarian questioned.

"I'll try to calm him, but he won't like it when you have to stick a needle in him."

Diana tried to calm Zephyr as much as possible. The team took about half an hour to examine him and get their blood sample. Diana tried talking to Zephyr to distract and calm him down as they injected him with an intravenous needle to extract blood. The wait for a sample of urine was longer.

The group used a long handle that held a cup at the end to catch some urine. Once they had all their results, they left without a word.

"How long are we going to have wait here?" Diana asked Sean. "It's almost ten o'clock already and the drive back to Allabrese takes hours."

"It could take another couple of hours," Sean sighed. "We'll have to wait as well."

"Curfew is at one o'clock," Diana said to him. "What if we miss it? Charlemagne would kill me."

"It'll be fine," Arturo replied. "I'm sure it will."

The three of them sat around for an hour, which then became two hours. Diana's head came up as she heard the screech of the P.A.

"Attention to our racers who have stuck around," a different voice said on the P.A. "Unfortunately, due to the detection of narcotics, one contender has been disqualified from the competition."

Diana looked up to the screen as it removed Bell Bell from the previous race. The graphics then switched to show the net provincial standings. Drop Down had still beaten Zephyr, but with Bell Bell eliminated from the competition, she was now in second place.

"Drop Down and Zephyr will be moving on to the final race in Allabrese," the P.A. announced.

"Yes!" Diana proclaimed. "Yes!"

Diana ran over to Zephyr and hugged him.

"Do you hear that?" Diana said to him. "We have another chance!"

"Thank God," Arturo remarked. "Congrats."

"What a stroke of luck," Sean replied. "Congratulations, kiddo. We're going to the finale."

Diana didn't reply and simply continued to hug Zephyr with a tight embrace. A tear ran down from her right eye as she smiled.

Act 5, Scene 2

Tristan kept trying to update his phone as he was being driven to the Huxley residence by Mavis. He was looking at news updates for the Calgary Stake. According to his phone, it was only about seven o'clock and the race wasn't to start for another hour. Tristan sighed.

"What's wrong, Master Tristan?" Mavis questioned.

"I shouldn't be going on this date," Tristan confessed. "I don't like this girl. I like Diana."

"Do you want me to turn around?"

"No," Tristan replied, "I have to do this because Peter would kill me if I canceled and it would crush her. I just need to do this, set the record straight, and that's that."

Mavis pulled into the driveway of the large home belonging to Richard Huxley. Tristan took a deep breath and exited the vehicle.

"I'll call you if I need to leave before ten o'clock," Tristan said. "Also, please don't say anything about this to Diana or Charlemagne. I don't want to hurt her feelings. I'm going to make things right with this girl and then focus on Diana."

"Very well. Best of luck," Mavis said as Tristan left.

Tristan closed the door behind him and walked forward to the front door of the house. The Huxley estate was a large house, but it wasn't as big as the Cabernet Manor. There was still daylight outside, but the sun was on course to set within the hour. Tristan walked to the door and knocked.

Peter answered the door and bumped fists with Tristan.

"Alright," Peter said, greeting him. "Let's go. I'm starving."

"Tristie!" Vivian exclaimed from atop of the staircase ahead. "I'm so excited for our date!"

Tristan gave a nervous smile as he looked to her. She was dressed in a casual yellow dress. She came down the stairs and hugged Tristan.

"Hi," Tristan awkwardly said to her, patting her on the back.

"Alright, you idiots ready? I have to pick up Maia on the way and then we go eat," Peter remarked, putting on his football jacket.

Tristan left with Vivian and Huxley, and the two walked over to the red SUV parked outside of the garage.

"You two can sit in the back," Peter said as they approached the car.

Tristan walked over to the car and opened the door for Vivian. She climbed in before him. Peter got into the driver's seat and then drove off. They left the house and drove into town before passing through. They came to another large estate on the outskirts, which was the Grayson residence.

Peter pulled up along the causeway of the house and got out. Tristan and Vivian were left alone.

"I'm so happy we could have this night together," Vivian said with a warm smile. "I know you're really busy with school and sports because you want to be a doctor like Peter, so this means a lot to me."

Tristan nodded to her.

"Is everything alright? You seem nervous," Vivian said.

"No, it's just that..." Tristan struggled to speak. "I don't know how to say this."

"It's okay," Vivian replied, bringing a hand over Tristan's. "I get it. You're nervous too."

Tristan closed his eyes and rolled them behind his eyelids. Peter returned with Maia, and she sat in the front seat with Peter. The car then sped off and went back downtown. He was quiet in the car while Peter and Maia chatted.

Peter drove them to a diner on the edge of downtown Allabrese. They parked outside and then all got out to go inside. They were then seated where the majority of conversation was kept up by the others with Tristan occasionally responding to direct communication towards him.

After the four of them ate, Tristan took out his phone and leaned his head against the glass window. He refreshed the standings for the Calgary Stake, but there was a delay due to a weak signal.

"So," Vivian said, putting a hand on Tristan's thigh, "Maia and I are just going to go to the washroom for a second. Is that okay?"

"Sure," Tristan quietly said, refreshing his phone again.

The girls left Tristan with Peter. Peter watched them leave while Tristan continued to look at his phone. Peter then turned to Tristan once they were gone.

"What the hell is wrong with you?" Peter scolded. "We're supposed to be on a double date here. Put your phone away and get your head out of your ass."

Tristan rolled his eyes and put his phone away.

"Listen, dude," Tristan said to him. "I need to confess something. I don't think it's going to work out between me and Vivian."

"Are you serious?"

"I am. I just... I don't find her attractive and she's really annoying. I'm sorry, but I'm only here to honor my commitment and set the record straight."

"You bastard," Peter responded. "How can you say that about my sister? You like her."

"I'm sorry, but I really don't. We just don't click, and I'm going to tell her that."

"You tell her this, and I'll tell the rest of the school that you're a faggot, Tristan," Peter threatened. "I'm serious about that, because you'd have to be a faggot to be saying what you're telling me."

Peter gave a serious look to Tristan before he turned to smile to Maia and Vivian as they returned. Tristan crossed his arms and looked back at Peter with a serious glare.

"Hey!" Vivian cheered.

"Did you miss us?" Maia asked.

"I missed you," Peter flirted, smiling at his girlfriend.

Tristan didn't say anything and instead moved aside so that Vivian could sit back next to him.

"I love how, like, retro this place is," Maia said, looking around. "I mean, I feel like we're actually in the fifties."

"Oh, come on, who would want to go back to the fifties?" Peter replied. "You know?"

"Tristan," Vivian said, looking at him, "I have an idea for where we can go for our next date."

"Huh?" Tristan questioned.

"Where?" Peter interrupted. "I'm sure Tristan is dying to know."

"We should go to the county fair!" Vivian suggested. "I heard that it's going to be back this May."

Tristan didn't respond.

"I think that's a great idea!" Maia replied. "All four of us should go – it'd be so much fun!"

"Yeah, isn't that a great idea?" Peter asked, looking to Tristan.

"Vivian..." Tristan said, unfolding his arms.

"How are you all doing?" their waitress asked, presenting the bill. "I'm just going to leave this here. Take your time, there's no rush."

"Thank you," Tristan replied as she took their plates.

The waitress then left.

"Oh, I have another idea if everybody is up for it next Sunday. My dad gave me tickets to the Nattau Derby finals next Sunday. They're VIP tickets too and came from the owner of that place."

"Ooh! Horse racing sounds fun!" Vivian smiled. "Tristan, isn't your sister racing in that?"

"Yeah, she is," Tristan replied, giving a worried look. "She's been kicking ass, but I haven't been to any of her races yet. She's also racing today in Calgary."

"Wow, I think that's the most I've heard you talk today," Peter remarked with a serious face.

"Oh, Tristan's just a good listener," Vivian defended him, "and you know, that's really something that's hard to find nowadays."

Peter and Tristan glared at each other.

"You know, I'm surprised that sister of yours actually did something with her life," Peter remarked. "There's something seriously messed up with that girl."

"No, that's only you," Tristan replied.

The table went quiet as Tristan and Peter continued to look at each other.

"Uh, Tristie," Vivian interrupted. "I'm having trouble with my math homework. Do you think you could come over one day to help me out?"

"Uh, I don't know," Tristan responded. "I really busy, and there's actually something I want to talk to you about."

"Come on, Tristan," Peter motivated. "Why don't you want to help out my sister? Only a faggot would refuse to help her out."

"Why don't you help her out then?" Tristan barked back.

"Whoa, take it easy there, tiger," Peter sarcastically responded. "There's not need to take it personally."

"Can you help me?" Vivian asked again in a cute voice.

"I don't know, Vi," Tristan replied, annoyed.

The table went quiet again.

"So, where are we going next?" Maia chimed in.

"Well, Tristan and I had agreed to take you to the drive-in theater," Peter said. "They're showing tonight."

"Oh, what time?" Maia asked.

"I think it starts at about nineish," Peter replied, looking at his watch. "We should start to head out, actually."

Tristan took out some money and set it on the table. He then crossed his arms again and looked at Peter as he took out his car keys.

"Uh, Maia and I are going to handle the bill. Why don't you take Tristan back to my car and, uh... warm it up a little?" Peter said, smiling at Maia.

"Sure thing!" Vivian replied, grabbing the keys and then standing up. "Come on, Tristie!"

Vivian offered Tristan her hand, but he refused it as he slid himself out from the booth and stood up on his own. He walked with her out of the restaurant and they went back to Peter's SUV.

"Here," Vivian said, giving him the keys. "You can sit in the driver's seat since you're the man."

Tristan took the keys and unlocked the car. He then went and sat in the front while Vivian went around to sit next to him.

"Do you think they'll take long?" Tristan asked as he put the keys in the cup holder.

"Let's hope so," Vivian replied, pressing her hand against Tristan's thigh.

"Whoa, what are you doing?" Tristan questioned, jerking his thigh up out of reflex.

"What do you mean?" Vivian questioned. "Am I doing something wrong?"

Tristan sighed and looked at her. She then kissed him, forcing herself onto him as he tried to push her back.

"Stop!" Tristan yelled. "I'm sorry, but we need to talk."

"What? Talk about what?"

"About us," Tristan said to her. "I'm sorry, but we can't see each other."

"What? Why?"

Tristan didn't immediately respond.

"I'm sorry," Tristan instead said. "I'm just... I'm just not attracted to you."

"What? You're joking, right?"

"No," Tristan asserted in his annoyed tone. "I'm... I'm just sorry, okay."

"Tristan..." Vivian replied in a sad tone. "Was I too forward? You seem upset. I want to know what's wrong... Please, tell me."

"I'm sorry, Vivian," Tristan replied. "You are a nice girl, but you're not for me."

Vivian looked at him in horror. Her eyes watered.

"I thought you liked me..." Vivian responded. "All those times you cat-called me, and I ignored you, and now.... and now you're breaking up with me?!"

"I'm not breaking up with you," Tristan responded. "We were never dating in the first place."

Vivian opened her mouth in shock. Tristan's phone vibrated. He picked it up and looked at it, but Vivian brought her hand over to stop him.

"Hey, bug off!" Tristan replied, brushing her hand away.

"Excuse me?!"

Tristan opened the car door and got out. He then read the text message sent to him from Charlemagne, which said, 'Tristan –

where are you? Do you know where Diana is? I just talked to the community center, and they were closed. Where is she?'

"Crap..." Tristan whispered, swiping to unlock his phone.

Tristan replied to Charlemagne and said, 'Sorry, I'm with Peter. I don't know where Diana is, but I thought she was with Arturo?'

"Tristan Merrick, you come back here!" Vivian shouted, slamming the car door from behind her.

Tristan looked to the side as she saw her come around. She tried to swipe Tristan's phone from his hand.

"Who's the other girl?! Who?!" she shouted.

"Vivian, calm down," Tristan said to her. "You're going to draw attention to us."

"I hope I draw attention to us, because I want them to look at the man who turned me down for some whore!"

Tristan frowned at her. He then looked back at his phone as it vibrated. Charlemagne had responded to his message and said, 'Is Diana racing in the Nattau Derby? I just asked Richard and he thought I knew.'

"Oh no," Tristan muttered, putting his phone away.

"Tristan!" Vivian shouted.

"Shut up," Tristan replied, looking back at her. "I'm sorry, but it's over between us. Please, don't talk to me ever again. I have to go."

"You come back here!" Vivian yelled as Tristan walked off and past the entrance of the diner.

Peter stormed out of the diner and grabbed Tristan before he could leave. Maia followed behind him.

"Get off me!" Tristan yelled, pushing him away.

"Who is the other woman!" Vivian yelled from the parking lot.

"I'm giving you one chance, Merrick," Peter threatened. "You have one chance to make this right again."

"I'm sorry, but I can't," Tristan replied, pushing him back. "I have to go."

"Who's the whore?!" Vivian yelled again.

Tristan and Peter looked at each other.

"It's not a whore," Peter shouted to his sister. "It's a boy – a faggot. You see, that's why Tristan has to go. It's because he has a boy toy waiting for him somewhere else. I wonder who it is too. Who's the man that gets to peg you in the ass and leave you so butt hurt all the time?"

"I'll kill you!" Tristan shouted, tackling Peter onto the ground.

Vivian and Maia caught up to them and yelled in horror.

"Oh my God, Peter!" Maia cried out.

"Tristan, stop!" Vivian pleaded.

Tristan punched Peter across the face before they started to block each other's hands and arms. Peter eventually punched Tristan back, letting him stand up.

Tristan covered his nose as blood poured down. He then grabbed Peter and bashed him against the diner window. He threw a punch at him, which caused him to sit down on the ground. Tristan spat at him before deciding to walk off.

"We're done, Huxley," Tristan said to him. "Goodbye."

"Yeah, that's right," Peter remarked, spitting out his own blood. "Run... but I'm not done, Merrick. You are. You're finished."

Tristan ignored him and continued down the street.

"You're done!" Peter yelled. "F. A. G. G. O. T. – faggot. That's you, Merrick! A complete faggot with a capital F. Go on and run off to your toy! The whole school is going to know about it!"

Tristan continued to ignore him and walk away until he couldn't hear him anymore. Eventually, the sound of Peter's taunts were too far away to be able to hear, letting Tristan take a deep breath as he walked back home.

Act 5, Scene 3

"Where is she?" Charlemagne questioned as he paced around the foyer of the manor.

The front door opened and Tristan walked inside with soaked hair.

"Sorry I took so long, but I had to walk home," Tristan said to her. "It also started to rain in the last twenty minutes, and I didn't bring a coat."

"Where is she?" Charlemagne yelled. "I want to know where she is! On Friday, I got strange text messages about her competing in the Nattau Derby, and I didn't believe them until I started to receive texts from people giving me condolences for her apparent loss in Calgary. Calgary!"

"What? She lost?" Tristan replied. "I- I mean, I didn't know she was playing, but if she was, I'm surprised she didn't win..."

"Is there something you should be telling me?" Charlemagne questioned, walking over to him. "Where is she?"

"I swear, I don't know," Tristan replied. "I don't know anything, but why are you mad? Maybe she likes this hobby of hers. You told her to reach out into the community and involve herself. Maybe this is her activity? Maybe she likes this? Maybe it makes her happy? Can you be mad about it?"

"I'm not mad if this is her interest," Charlemagne corrected him. "I'm mad that she's gone behind my back and defied me. I told her to be careful around that place, especially the man who tricked my father out of that equestrian center. The only reason why he won was because he doped the horse that he pushed to race against his. I know because I went to the trouble of getting a blood sample to test it for performance-enhancing substances, which he tested positive for. Of course, there were a mass of technicalities that prevented me from submitting this blood as actual evidence, my *passive* father told me to forget about it, and by the time any actual authorities could investigate, it was too late. When it comes to Barney Cohen, the man gets what he wants whenever he wants. He is a fraud and a cheat."

"Where is she now?" Tristan asked as if he didn't already know.

"Calgary," Charlemagne said. "Apparently, she lost the race there and I'm now waiting for her to shamelessly walk in here. Oh, but I have a surprise for her. I'm going to put down the hammer on her and assert myself."

Tristan didn't respond.

"Oh, I can only imagine what scheme and lies that pig has spilt to manipulate her into doing his bidding," Charlemagne said. "Diana isn't a racer. The last time she rode a horse, it ran away from her."

"It's between a four to six hours drive from here to Calgary," Tristan said to Charlemagne. "If you're constantly going the limit and not stopping that is."

"The race ended at nine o'clock, which means she won't be here until midnight. What was her plan? Did she think I wouldn't notice? Did she think that I'd be so negligent?"

Tristan didn't respond. He looked at his phone. It was only about ten o'clock.

"If she leaves after the race that is…"

"Oh, I've considered that too!" Charlemagne replied. "What's worse is that this is a school night. You should go to bed."

"I'm waiting here," Tristan declared.

"Do not undermine my authority too! Go to bed!" Charlemagne barked.

Tristan looked at him in his rage and decided to comply. He stood up and went upstairs, but did not go to bed. He stayed in his room and waited. Charlemagne continued to stay in the foyer for Diana.

At almost three o'clock at night, Diana looked at the time above the car radio. She was in Sean's SUV, sitting in the backseat as she was formerly with Arturo. Arturo had already been dropped off at this point. Sean made the trip across the bridge and then turned to come to the mansion. He stopped outside and looked over to Diana from the rear-view mirror.

"Try not to beat yourself up over the loss," Sean said. "Just relax and take it easy. Look forward, and be grateful of this comeback. We're still in this."

"Yeah, I'm more worried about whether Charlemagne is awake right now to be thinking about what happened. I'm exhausted too."

"Take it easy," Sean said to her. "Zephyr is a rough horse to ride and it's your talent to be able to ride him. I fear that after the loss today, Barney might approach you asking to cheat for the final. Do not let him tempt you or convince you that this is a good idea."

"I won't let him anywhere near my horse."

"That's the spirit," Sean replied.

"Let me take Zephyr in tonight," Diana also said as she opened her door. "I'll take him to the stables here and keep him company. I don't trust Barney anymore after what I've seen of him tonight."

"A wise idea," Sean replied, parking the car.

Sean exited the vehicle and went behind to the trailer to help Diana retrieve Zephyr. Diana walked him out and then looked over to Sean.

"Thanks," Diana said to him. "I'll see you tomorrow for training."

"Sure thing," Sean replied. "Have a goodnight."

Zephyr gave a light neigh as Sean went back to his SUV and then drove off. Diana led Zephyr around to the stables via the same route she took when she first snuck him in.

Charlemagne looked out from the foyer and followed her with his eyes. He then closed the curtain and continued to wait.

Diana led Zephyr into his old stall. She then closed the gate and climbed up to look in.

"I'll see you tomorrow, bud," Diana said. "Well, I mean later today. I don't blame you for what happened tonight. I blame myself. I was distracted. I shouldn't have pushed you so hard at the start of that race too. I'll sort myself out with Tristan, and then we can have a good race next Sunday, okay?"

Zephyr turned to her in his stall. He gave a light huff before Diana patted him on the side of his head.

"I'll see you later, okay?" Diana said, dropping down. "I love you."

Diana left the barn with a smile on her face. She walked down the causeway from the garage and went around to the front door. She saw lights on and walked up to open the door with her satchel around her back. She unlocked it and then pushed forward.

Tristan left his room and went to the foyer as he saw Charlemagne stand up and Diana enter. He stopped by the railings.

"Diana!" Tristan shouted.

"Tristan, go back to your room at once!" Charlemagne shouted, turning around before looking back to Diana. "Where the bollocks have you been, young lady!"

"What do you mean?" Diana replied, dropping her smile. "I was at the rec center, remember?"

"It's three o'clock in the morning and it is Sunday night. Do you expect me to believe your lies?" Charlemagne replied. "I know the truth. I know you're racing for that swine, Barney Cohen! I've heard everything I need to from everybody, because it appears that I'm the only fool who hasn't known."

Diana frowned. She began to breath at a steady, but deep beat. Her hands trembled and she avoided looking at Tristan. She focused her eyes on Charlemagne instead.

"You're two hours over your generous curfew. What were you thinking in deceiving me like this?! Did you really think I wouldn't find out sooner or later?! I'm sorry, but I simply cannot tolerate this rebellious behavior. I understand and have observed that you're depressed. I understand that because you're a teenager, but I'm sorry. I simply cannot put up with this. I will not have you racing for that swine. I will not have you place yourself in the face of danger. Do you have any idea what you were doing?"

"Yeah, I do," Diana responded with attitude, tensing her hands as she made a fist.

"Where did you even get on with this horse racing? What scheme did he shove down your throat to convince you to race with him? Do you not understand that it's not about talent, but that he manipulates everything? He chooses the winners beforehand by drugging the horse he wants to win. It's not about skill. He deceives you into thinking you have skill."

Diana's frown worsened.

"My horse isn't on drugs," Diana replied in a weak voice. "They just did a drug test today and they found nothing."

"Cohen is the one that pays for these people to test the horses! Do you not think that they're in his pockets too? You see, you do not understand how deep the rabbit hole goes with these sort of matters. Your naiveté has you trust these crooked people on an ideal that they're good people, but they're not, Diana. They're bad people."

"I understand that bad people exist in the world!" Diana shouted.

"And let's not forget about your behavior in general," Charlemagne ranted. "I've received multiple phone calls from teachers about your performance. I've received your interim report card for April. You're failing three of your classes, and here I was, like an idiot, making excuses for you when you're behind my back doing this nonsense! How do you go from being an excellent student to being the worst I have ever seen?!"

"Charles," Tristan interrupted in a loud voice.

Charlemagne turned to him with a red face. Diana looked at Tristan with angry eyes.

"I told you to go to your room! If you continue to defy me too, I will have you sent to military school!"

Charlemagne then turned back to Diana. She had a deep frown on her face.

"As for you, your actions have exhausted me. I thought we had set ourselves clear in July, and I have no other options at this point. I've accepted you into this home. I've sheltered you, given you food, and I've given you a considerable amount of freedom, but you've disrespected me and broken my trust, and I'm afraid I have no other choice but- but to have you possibly removed…"

"Do it then!" Diana shouted to him. "Do it and set me free!"

Charlemagne stepped back from her sudden outburst.

"I would appreciate it because right now, I need you to leave me the hell alone! I don't give a damn about my grades! I don't give a damn about this house! I just want to be in peace! In peace! Please, please, just leave me alone!"

Diana turned around and started to open the door.

"Where are you going?!" Charlemagne complained.

"Diana, wait!" Tristan yelled, rushing down the stairs.

Diana turned to him as he was about to approach her.

"Get the hell away from me!" Diana shouted, pointing at him. "Don't you ever talk to me ever again, do you hear me! I knew you didn't care about me! You're nothing but a selfish traitor – I can't believe I let my guard down – I can't believe I trusted you!"

Diana took a step back and shook her head. Tristan could see tears forming at the cusp of her eyes. She ran off as it started to rain again.

"No, Diana!" Tristan yelled, rushing outside.

"Where do you think you're going too!" Charlemagne remarked, grabbing him.

"What are you doing?!" Tristan responded, brushing him off. "Let go of me! You're letting her get away."

Tristan violently pushed Charlemagne off of him before he could run down the steps, barefoot and bare-chested in the rain. He ran down the driveway and looked over to where he saw Diana enter the garage. He then ran after her. Charlemagne ran after both of them.

Diana entered the garage, ran over to open the garage door into the pen, and then went to Zephyr's stall to open the gate. She then entered the stall as Tristan entered the garage.

"Diana, please!" Tristan yelled to her as she climbed atop of Zephyr.

Diana rode Zephyr out of his stall and down the aisle. Zephyr reared at Tristan, causing him to fall backwards. Zephyr then ran into the pen where he jumped over the fence. Tristan got up and ran into the muddy pen. Diana and Zephyr went around and then disappeared from his view. Tristan turned around and went back out the front garage door. He ran back down the causeway where he saw Charlemagne change direction as they both saw Diana riding away from the house and going towards the road.

The duo disappeared into the rain and darkness, and both Tristan and Charlemagne stood helplessly.

"Oh dear," Charlemagne said in a quiet voice. "I believe I was a little too hard on her..."

"Oh, you think?" Tristan replied with a weak voice.

Tristan's face was wet with both rain water and tears as he tried to see Diana through the darkness.

Diana galloped away from the mansion and made her way up the on-ramp that merged onto the highway. She rode Zephyr down the Nattau Bridge, crossed the river, and sped along with her horse and no sense of direction. She rode all the way to the Allabrese Equestrian Center where she stopped outside of the main entrance and hopped off. Diana walked over to a payphone and inserted some coins. She then dialed a number and hoped to hear a response.

After a minute, no response came. She slammed the phone and tried again, but no response came. Instead, it went to voicemail.

"Arturo, it's me, Diana," Diana said in a weak voice. "I- I need somewhere to go tonight. I- I got into a fight with Charlemagne. I shouted at Tristan. A lot of stuff has happened today, and I just need somewhere to go tonight. Please, please, help me. I hope you hear this because I really need somewhere to go with Zephyr. If you hear this, I'll be near the equestrian center with him. Please, help us out."

Diana put the phone down and then brought her forehead against the booth. She pushed herself away and then walked over to Zephyr. The two walked together away from the building and down the dirt path along the side of the large fenced pasture. They then walked around and came to the bank of the river.

The rain started to settle as they reached the water. She found a tree to sit against and look out into the darkness. She then brought her knees to her chest as Zephyr came down next to her. She pet him and the two stood there for a couple of hours. Eventually, Diana fell to her side closest to Zephyr and went to sleep. Zephyr kept his head near her and stayed awake, keeping watch.

Diana woke up as she felt Zephyr move. She looked around her and saw that it was twilight and a light rain in the air. The sky was cloudy with pink patches above. She turned to her side where Zephyr was looking at as he stood up.

"Easy," Arturo said to him. "I'm a friend."

"Art," Diana greeted, standing up and going to him. "You came."

Diana rushed over to Arturo. He was wearing a black poncho over his clothes despite the fact that his black hair was wet. She hugged him. He removed his poncho and gave it to her. He also removed his sweater and passed it to her.

"I have a spare with me," Arturo said to her.

"I'm already wet," Diana replied.

"Mine is warm and you don't need to get anymore wet than you are," Arturo reasoned. "Come on, let's get you back to my place."

Diana took both. She removed her wet sweater and then put on Arturo's. She then brought the poncho over. She put her wet sweater in her satchel.

Arturo walked over to the horse above the ledge. Arturo's horse looked like a unicorn with its clean white-coat and silver hair. He retrieved another poncho and put it on. He then brought a rope and gave it to her.

"Can you put this around Zephyr's neck so he can follow us?" Arturo asked.

"Sure," Diana replied, taking the rope and then walking over to Zephyr.

Diana put the rope around his neck like a necklace and then led him over to Arturo and his horse. He mounted his horse and took the rope. He then helped Diana onto the back of his horse. She put her arms around his waist and held on.

Arturo started to walk away from the river bank, leading Zephyr away with Diana on the back of his horse. She rested against his back and began to close her eyes as they started to move. Within a couple of minutes, she was asleep again.

Act 5, Scene 4

Diana opened her eyes and looked forward to where she saw light pouring in through the cracks of some blinds. She was on her side. There was an end table next to her, and immediately next to this table was a row of three windows with further windows on the adjacent wall. The windows were arched and had a caramel-colored frame. They also had transparent terracotta curtains that were pulled over. Diana pushed herself from the bed she was on.

The sheets of the bed were grey and the cover was an aubergine-colored quilt. The frame of the bed was a dark brown wood. Diana came onto her back and then sat up. She looked around the room and saw that on the full-sized bed she was in, she was alone.

"Hello?" Diana questioned.

The room she was in was L-shaped. She tried to look around the corner to see if there was someone with her. She finally got out of bed and looked around, seeing the couch against the wall and desk on the other side. The floors of the room were a wooden patterned floorboard and the walls were painted in a goldenrod color. Under the bed and around the corner were rugs in the same color as the curtains. By the desk there was a guitar.

Diana sat back down at the bed and looked to the end table on the opposite side from where she had slept. A smartphone was lying there, charging. Diana picked it up and looked at the time. It was almost two o'clock in the afternoon. She put the phone back and then stood up. She was wearing the same sweater that Arturo gave her when he found her. She walked over to the windows and started to open the blinds on each of them.

When Diana found the blinds for the door going out to the balcony patio surrounding the perimeter of the bedroom, she pulled it up and opened the door to step out. There was a humid breeze reaching the patio as it was a warm spring day. She could see around the Medici property from where she was. Below, she could see the large pool with its light blue water and surrounding patio before the large gardens that extended around. The sun was out and there wasn't a cloud in the sky. Diana moved over to the other side of the patio where there was a large pasture and a barn nearby.

Near the barn, Diana could see Arturo brushing the white horse he had ridden. Zephyr was nearby, but not too close to them. He was eating some grass on the pasture. Arturo wore nothing more than black boots and a pair of jeans. Diana focused her eyes on him. The boy had physique similar to Tristan, who had grown since last autumn, and like him wore a gold necklace; a Venetian gold chain necklace, but with a Christian cross rather than an amulet. Diana took notice because Arturo had not worn that necklace before, or rather, she had not taken notice up to this point but was sure he had not worn it.

Diana stepped away from the railings of the balcony and entered Arturo's bedroom. She then walked around to the staircase and came downstairs. From the second floor, she walked down the corridor of the manor, passing some housekeepers to go to the foyer. She then navigated to the rear of the house to step down onto a gravel path. Diana then made her way around to the pasture where she looked over to Arturo and the horses with crossed arms and a neutral expression.

Arturo looked up and over to her as she came closer. He stopped brushing his horse and walked over to a table against the barn where his dress shirt was. He then put it on, but didn't button it up. He walked past his horse and over to Diana.

"Hey, I'm glad you're awake," Arturo said to her. "Are you hungry?"

Diana shrugged.

"You should eat something – I'll make you something. Come, and then we can talk about what happened."

Arturo led Diana back inside and to the kitchen. He sat her down at the kitchen island on a stool and then started to fetch ingredients from around the large kitchen. The Medici kitchen was larger than the Cabernet kitchen. It was about double the size. Arturo prepared some crepes with fruits at the side for Diana and then brought them over to her. He then sat next to her.

Diana ate and explained what happened after she got home. She explained what Charlemagne said to her and that she knew Tristan betrayed her. She also said that she doesn't want to return to the mansion but said that she doesn't want to stay here in Medici Manor.

"Where are you going to go?" Arturo questioned. "You can't go anywhere else."

"I have – options," Diana replied. "I- I don't even know if I want to participate in the final race. I shouldn't. I didn't deserve to make it to the final round after the humiliating loss I had."

"You're being overly negative," Arturo said to her. "Charlemagne was a little harsh, but you need to make amends with him. He won't kick you out. He's not heartless."

"I don't want to go back though," Diana replied. "Tristan… I don't want to look at him ever again and I don't want to look at Charles ever again."

Arturo frowned at her but then raised a smile.

"You missed school today," Arturo said to her.

"Shucks," Diana replied. "Well, that's just too darn bad."

Arturo gave her a look of disbelief and then stood up.

"What's her name?" Diana asked. "Your horse?"

"Misty," Arturo replied. "She's not my horse. She's the family horse."

"I didn't realize you could ride horses or such," Diana said to her.

"It's the country," Arturo explained. "And we have the money to support her and have her here. Do you want to go for a ride?"

"A ride?"

"Yeah, just take the horses out around outside. There's a river ahead that's nice to go to," Arturo said, "plus, they can use the exercise since they've been around here all day."

"Sure," Diana replied, "let's go for a ride."

Arturo took Diana's plate and put it in the sink.

"I need to shower beforehand though," Diana said to him. "I didn't get to when I got home, and I smell awful."

Diana and Arturo split up with Diana going upstairs to shower in Arturo's bathroom while he went back outside. She showered quickly and got dressed in the same clothing. She then went downstairs and outside to join him where he was.

Arturo was holding a hose and pouring water into a trough so the horses could drink. They sloshed on some water and then were mounted by their respective owners. Arturo rode off from the barn and went down to the pasture. Diana followed and tried to catch up. Arturo saw her trying to catch up, smiled and sped Misty up.

Diana saw what he was doing and got Zephyr to speed forward. Soon, the two horses were galloping next to each other down along the grass field towards an oak forest. Arturo slowed his horse down and pulled her aside, trudging off another direction, causing Diana to stop and readjust to follow him.

Arturo laughed as he did so and Diana smiled. She rushed over to him and tried to push him off from his horse. Arturo did the same, but neither of them succeeded in this dangerous act. Arturo led Diana to a trail through the forest and she followed him from behind. The horses trotted forward at a light pace.

At the end of the trail, Arturo made a U-turn and stopped in front of Diana so he could face her. He then quickly ran down the trail before they came to the edge of a narrow river at the sides of some steep banks. The two continued to ride down along the side of it until the ground smoothed out and the creek widened. On the other side of the creek was a large vineyard that stretched around with a barn up ahead.

The water was clear in the stream and one could see the fish and rocks at the bottom of the shallow body of water. Arturo continued to lead Diana down the river where she saw a wooden bridge ahead. The two continued to the bridge, crossed it, and then went down a grassy path towards the beach of a wide river that was like a large pond with trees behind, leaves flowing with the wind. Arturo slowed down and stopped there. He got off Misty and looked towards the water. Diana got off Zephyr and stepped down.

The area around them was extremely quiet with the only sound being the birds and the insects chirping away. A dragonfly passed them as they made their way towards a dock on the side of the water. Arturo stopped at the dock and sat down. He took off his shoes and then brought his feet into the water. Diana sat down next to him but crossed her legs.

"You know, it's really beautiful around here," Diana admitted. "I've never seen this much beauty outdoors in my life."

"Of course," Arturo replied. "You grew up and were raised in the city. What kind of nature do they have there? Pigeons? Parks? I thought it was about time somebody brought you out to see what the countryside is truly about. My ancestors have lived here for almost three-hundred years since we came to the *Pianure Calbresi* (Calabrese Plains), or as it's more commonly known, Champion Plains. The river we're at is called the *Carella Ruscello*, or just the Carella," he explained, taking a deep breath as he inhaled the fresh air around him. "I've lived around this my entire life, you know. I wouldn't want to have lived anywhere else than here, because here it's so quiet and peaceful... I'm lucky to be able to live here."

"What are you trying to achieve in showing me all this beauty behind your house?" Diana questioned him.

"Nothing," Arturo replied, "but you've had such a stressful season. I thought it would be a nice change of pace to bring you here. Maybe to try and convince you that there's nothing to live for in a city like Harlech, and that you should stay here?"

"Aren't you going to go to Harlech?" Diana asked. "For school?"

"Yeah," Arturo sighed, "but that's pending an answer from a special girl in my life."

Diana didn't reply.

"A special girl who should go back to her guardian and apologize."

"Apologize? I'm not apologizing to him!" Diana replied.

Arturo sighed and looked out to the water. Behind the two of them, Misty and Zephyr were approaching each other. Diana looked at them and gave a light smile. She uncrossed her arms and brought a hand down onto Arturo's. She then looked at him and he looked into her eyes. Arturo then kissed her.

The couple spent the afternoon by the river until Arturo took his feet from the water and walked with Diana to the field. Zephyr and Misty had wandered away as Diana and Arturo came to the field and laid down in the grass, looking up to the sky.

Diana held Arturo's arm as she they lay together with their backs to the grass. The two started to cloud gaze together.

"Can I ask you some questions?" Diana suddenly said in their silence.

"Sure."

"What kind of people were your parents?"

"My parents…" Arturo replied, sighing. "Why?"

"I want to know what kind of people they were," Diana responded. "It's as simple as that."

"Well," Arturo answered, "my mom was sweet and caring. She was the type of woman who would make any sacrifice for her children. She would cook for me, buy me things, and just do things for me that I would never expect or ask from her. You know, the fondest memory I have of her is when I was about six-years old and she read to me when I was in bed. She read to me in Italian too, from a picture book about a duck. I treasure that memory close to my heart."

"Wow, that's beautiful," Diana replied. "And your dad?"

"He was great too," Arturo answered. "You know, you and the rest of the world outside this mansion might think of Giovanni Medici as a cold and bitter mobster, but as my dad, he cared about his kids. He spent a lot of time with me, playing sports, teaching me to ride a horse and a bike, to swim, and all other activities. He disciplined me. He taught me to be my best. He was a great man, but he had a lot of conflict…"

"And how was he with your mom?"

"They were a power couple," Arturo replied. "The two of them loved each other so much. Every single time he would return home, even if it was to step out for a bit, he would return to her and kiss her. You know, before he died, he spent a lot of time in hiding and it hurt him a lot because of the fact he was separated from both us and my mom. He hated being away from us. The man didn't idolize us. He just cared about us deeply and we were special to him. My dad idolized my mom though. He had so much passion for her and would die for her."

"That's sweet…" Diana replied. "You had a good example set before you."

"Yeah, I did," Arturo agreed. "It's important for kids to have that in their mom and dad."

Diana paused for a moment before she looked to Arturo again.

"Why do you want to go into business?" Diana questioned. "Besides to take over the family business?"

"I want to set things right," Arturo answered. "I thought my nonno was a great man once. After he died, I did all I could to try and learn about him. I heard both terrible and amazing things about him, and I saw him as a fearless leader that didn't crack at pressure. You see, Medici used to be more than just construction. We used to own a chain of banks across the world known as The Bank of Medici. It was founded by my ancestor, Romano Medici, who was from this very town. Italians have been in Allabrese for more time than the English, who came here as Catholic exiles. He made his business with the fur traders, holding their riches for them, and through this service his influence grew and he was able to branch out, going to Montreal, New York, and as far back as into Italy. We had an empire, but then we became a black nobility, which meant we had allegiance to the Pope during the *Risorgimento*, and because of that, we were forced out from Italy for almost sixty-years when the Pope lost his power. In that time, we focused our business here, in the New World, but it hurt us. In this time, my great-great-grandfather, Augusto, took absolute control and led us through the hard times. Later we received compensation thanks to Mussolini for what we lost, but even then, the company continued to decline because it was too large and too much to manage for that time period. There was a lot of corruption. My nonno, Nero, found himself at a point where he could have made reforms to save the company, but instead of solving the problems, he gave in to them. He lost it all and my papa was left with nothing. The house we live in now – that used to be one of many resort homes we owned. It's all we really have left. The entire empire crumbled, and Cabernet Industries was one of the many companies that benefited from our decline in the sixties."

"So, what do you want to do?"

"I want to bring us back to greatness," Arturo replied, "no matter what that might look like, I want to restore the honor and trust in the Medici family name, which was salted by my nonno. It… it's a rendition of my father's old dream, but he was stuck between the old ways of his papa, Nero, because he was raised under them, and creating his own. I want to do what both of them could never do. I know I can do it."

"How? I mean, I don't know much about economics and business, but it seems like in this day and age, creating a billion dollar empire is impossible due to the nature of the markets unless you can push yourself into a new market entirely."

"I know, but it doesn't have to be vast," Arturo replied. "It only has to be wholesome and powerful. Like Cabernet Industries. Charlemagne has influenced a lot in me, and I want to create a corporation that doesn't compete with his but holds its own niche and is like Cabernet Industries – to be partners."

"What's Charlemagne done to influence you? He's not a businessman. He owns his family business, but he hardly interferes. The people around him do all the work, and he approves of it."

"Charlemagne is a tremendous leader! He has passion! He has strength and character! He saved my life!"

"Wait, what?"

Arturo paused for a moment.

"He- he saved my life," Arturo replied.

Arturo told Diana about the incident where Nero kidnapped him, possessed him, and then held him hostage in the cemetery last Halloween eve.

"Why haven't I heard of this?" Diana complained. "Why didn't Charles tell me about this on the ride home from the Halloween party or anytime afterwards?"

"I'm surprised you didn't know…" Arturo responded. "Did he ever tell you who killed my parents?"

"No, why?"

Arturo didn't reply. He had a frown on his face and he wasn't looking at the clouds.

"Who killed them?" Diana asked.

Arturo didn't reply.

"Art," Diana complained. "Who killed them?"

Arturo finally looked back up to the sky.

"I killed them," Arturo confessed. "I murdered them out of the frustration and delusion that flowed through me."

"What the hell? Even for you, that's a little morbid of a joke," Diana replied, looking at him. "Who really killed them?"

"I told you, after my nonno died, I started to indulge myself in false knowledge about him. I worshiped him. I idolized him. I wanted to be like him, and he told me to kill the weak liability that was his son. He blamed his son for his losses and his failures when it was really his own losses and failures. So, I entered their bedroom and killed them."

"That's horrible," Diana replied, sitting up. "You're a murderer! All this time, I thought you were depressed because they were dead, but you're depressed because they're dead *and* you killed them!"

"The manipulation of that old fool was enough to get me to do anything," Arturo said to her in a cold tone. "I have a vague memory of the actual incident, but there are glimpses and parts that have come back to me when I sleep, which is really the reason why I can't sleep at all. I can hear some screams, some pleading, and also the gunshots and blood. If it weren't for Charlemagne finding me in that closet and talking to me, I probably would have killed myself with the same gun because when I came to, I was horrified with what I did and couldn't believe it. Charlemagne was nice and understanding though. He knew I wasn't in control of my own actions, and he and Dino covered it up for me to keep me safe."

"Charles knew about this too!" Diana questioned. "Oh my God, Art, this is horrible!"

"I'm sorry," Arturo confessed, sitting up as tears rolled down his cheeks. "I shouldn't have told you, but it's the last secret I really have to share with you. It's all I have, and I don't think I could do that again with anyone."

Diana looked at him and then looked to the side.

"I- I don't even know if I could have done the same to my own dad who I despised," Diana commented. "To kill your own blood in addition to killing in general. Oh my God, Art, I should be apologizing to you. I had no idea this is how deep it goes for you. You by far have it worse than me, and... you seem fine considering it. I mean, you're still depressive, but for what you did, you should be a mess. I didn't realize you were this strong all this time."

"All that keeps me moving forward is trying to make things right again," Arturo said. "To realize a dream that my father would have been proud of. To continue the Medici name for the sake of my parents, and to push forward."

"And I can't let you ditch out on an opportunity to realize this dream," Diana said to him. "I'm sorry, Art, but you need to go to school in Harlech and get into the university that will help you build yourself as your ancestors once built your family and to ensure that mistakes aren't repeated. For the sake of your father and mother, please, go to this school and forget about me, please."

"Are you just saying that because of what you've learned?" Arturo questioned with suspicion.

"No," Diana denied, "after what I've just learned, I want to hug you, kiss you, and never leave your side, but I can't because I do need to leave your side. You need to go and do whatever it is you need to do to accomplish this aspiration. I'm- I'm just a woman. I can birth your kids and mother them, but that's that. The path to this goal of yours is in your hands only, and only you can realize it with every fiber of your plentiful strength, love, and wisdom, of which I know you have lots of because no regular boy could have gone through what you've been through and lived to tell me. You are a hero even at your age, Arturo, and you will grow and become a great man one day. I know it since you show promise of being one at only sixteen."

"If you want me to go to Harlech, then please, do me a favor too, Diana," Arturo asked. "Please, go back to Charlemagne and apologize to him. He's a good man and will forgive you. You have a good life in Allabrese, and you shouldn't miss out on this – all of this, for something so petty."

"I-"

"Please," Arturo insisted.

"Okay…" Diana replied, turning her head down in defeat. "I'll phone him."

"Thank you," Arturo responded, hugging her.

"But I want Zephyr to stay here until I can move him," Diana added. "He seems happy here with Misty, and I don't know what Charles might do to him so please take care of him until I can figure something out."

"Of course."

•

As the sun started to set, Diana walked down the front steps of the Medici Manor and towards the black car where Mavis was waiting. She opened the door for her and Diana sat inside with her satchel. Mavis then went around and entered the driver's seat.

"How mad is Charles?" Diana questioned as she started to drive back.

"Less angry than you anticipate," Mavis replied. "He was regretful over his own behavior and would like to speak with you. I'm sure you two will be able to work this out and carry on."

"Good," Diana remarked, looking out the window. "What about Tristan?"

"Tristan has been depressed all day today. I had to phone him in as being ill because he's been quite off."

Diana didn't respond. She simply looked out the car door and towards the many farms along the sides of the road back to the freeway as they went back to the manor.

Act 6, Scene 1

Diana exited the library of Cabernet Manor and started to make her way across the foyer when she heard the telephone ring. She stopped in the middle of the hallway and looked up towards the entrance into the north wing of the second floor. She then quickly went over to the telephone, grabbed it and then fled into the living room.

"Hello?" Diana questioned.

"Diana! Oh, it's about time I got through to you," Sean replied on the other end. "Where are you? You've missed all your training this week and the final race is about to begin in a couple hours?"

"I'm sorry, but I don't think I'll be able to make it," Diana confessed. "Charlemagne found out that I've been racing for Barney, and it got me in deep trouble. I- I had a hell of a night last Sunday and I've barely recovered one week later."

"You have to race," Sean reasoned. "You can't quit now at the final stretch."

"I already did it last race," Diana replied. "I might as well spare everybody their time."

"You can't quit."

"I'm sorry, but there's nothing I can do to circumvent this without running away, and to be honest, if I'm going to defy Charlemagne once more, it'll land me in so much trouble that I wouldn't bother or plan on returning."

Diana sighed.

"And it's not like I'd actually stand a chance even if I could race or wanted to race," Diana added. "The race is a scam because Barney drugs all the horses. I can't beat a bunch of horses on steroids."

"Not your horse," Sean replied. "Barney's men can't get even near Zephyr to touch him."

"I'm sorry, Sean, but I'm done. Goodbye."

Diana hung up on her coach and then took the phone back to the foyer. She then went upstairs and quietly passed the lab. From there, she went down the corridor, passing the gym where Tristan was inside.

Tristan saw Diana and dropped his weights. He then stormed out of the room and into the hall, following Diana back to her room. Diana tried to slam the door behind him, but he lodged his foot into the way so that she slammed the door against it.

"I'd appreciate it if you backed off," Diana said in an aggressive tone.

"Please, let me talk to you," Tristan begged. "We need to talk – I didn't rat you out."

"Oh, and I suppose Charlemagne magically found out about me racing then. He pressured you into telling the truth. Please, do me a favor and leave me alone for the next two years until I can get the hell out of this place. I have nothing to say to you, traitor."

"Diana…" Tristan replied with an anxious face.

"Leave me alone," Diana remarked, slamming the door against his foot. "Go away before you get me in trouble."

Tristan looked at her and gently retracted his foot. Diana then slammed the door closed. Tristan returned to the gym as the laboratory door ahead opened with Charlemagne stepping outside.

"What's all this noise?" Charlemagne questioned.

"Sorry, I dropped my weight set," Tristan replied. "I'll try to be quieter."

"No, it's quite alright," Charlemagne responded, returning to his room. "Carry on."

Tristan entered the gym and sat down at his bench. He ran his hand through his hair as he tilted his head down to look on the carpet.

Diana fixed her hair after closing the door on Tristan. She then walked over to her desk and opened the drawer to take out her box of cigarettes. She then walked into the bathroom and locked the door going into the gym. Diana opened the window and sat down on the side of the bathtub. She then lit a cigarette and proceeded to smoke it.

The day had a thickness of grey clouds with no sun poking out. Diana tried to look out the window, but her eyes wandered everywhere. She finished the cigarette before putting it out. She then tossed the bud out into the pen before closing the window. Diana then turned on the fan to the bathroom and went to her room before returning to the bathroom. She opened the carton of cigarettes and saw that there were none more left.

"Dammit," Diana complained, tossing the box into the garbage.

Diana returned to her room and opened her drawer. She rummaged around before finding several business cards she had stashed. She looked through each of them and stopped at the one with a buffalo on the front.

"Oh, crap…" Diana said, looking at the business card. "I completely forgot about this."

Diana looked at the address on the card and then turned it around to see the phone number. She set the card on her desk and looked at the time. It was almost seven o'clock in the afternoon. She looked around and then stepped over to her closet, opening it and retrieving her luggage.

"I have a little bit of hope left," Diana remarked under her breath. "He better be there still. I can be with them both – Scot and Art. To hell with this place."

Diana brought her luggage onto her bed and started to pack some of her clothing. She then found her backpack, took out all her school items and began to pack her laptop. Diana walked over to her dresser, opened the top right drawer, and then took out a large wad of bills. She took the money and put it in her backpack. Diana then returned to her dresser and looked up at the empty shelf which only had the picture frame of her and Tristan on its face next to another picture frame of her and Zephyr. She picked it up and looked at it once more, frowning.

"Traitor," she muttered, throwing the picture frame across her room.

The frame hit the wall and fell to the floor. The glass cracked. Diana sighed and picked up the other picture frame with her and Zephyr.

"At least he's in good hands now."

Diana took the picture of Zephyr and left it in her luggage. Once everything was packed, Diana walked over to her desk and picked up a school book. She opened it and tore a piece of paper. She then found a pencil and started to write. She left the paper on her desk before grabbing all her things. Diana turned off the fan in the bathroom before she went to the other door to leave, closing her bedroom door behind her.

Diana came to the main entrance, picked up the phone and then looked through a phonebook to pick out a taxi service. She dialed for them and then waited. Once the taxi arrived ten minutes later, she left the house and walked down the steps. She then opened the door for herself, brought her luggage in with her, and closed the door. She went down the hill of the mansion and towards the gates, opening them and then stepping out.

The driver stood outside of his taxi, opening the rear.

"Where to, miss?" the driver asked.

"The Broiled Buffalo," Diana ordered as she handed her luggage. "Please."

"The pub?"

"I don't plan on drinking," Diana scolded. "I'm meeting family there – even if I was, what business is it to you?"

"I'm sorry, miss."

The driver brought down the rear door and then went around to sit in the front. Diana took a back seat and looked at the mansion as they drove off, made a U-turn and then went back towards town. The taxi left Diana at the curb of the pub with her luggage. She picked up her things and started to walk up the steps of the pub. She then walked through the entrance and could catch a whiff of all the cigarette smoking seeping out.

A waitress in a black dress looked at Diana and stepped towards her.

"Hi," the waitress greeted. "Can I help you?"

"I'm looking for some friends," Diana said to her.

"Friends? In this place?" the waitress questioned. "I think you're lost."

"I'm sorry," Scot interfered from the side. "She's with us."

"Oh, well, here are your friends then," the waitress said, presenting Scot to her. "Please, enjoy your stay."

The woman walked off and left Diana with Scot. Scot looked at her.

"You were beginning to make me think that you weren't going to come," Scot said to her. "I'll take it by the suitcase that you're not just here to talk but have decided."

"Yeah, that's what the suitcase means," Diana replied.

"You have no idea how happy this makes me," Scot responded. "You certainly took your time in making a decision though."

"When can we leave?" Diana queried as they walked into the depths of the bar. "I want to leave as soon as possible."

"We can leave tonight if you'd like then," Scot replied. "We're only really here for you since we have no other business to attend to."

Scot took Diana to a round table in the corner of the bar. There, the leader of the syndicate was surrounded by various of his elite henchmen.

"Look who's decided to join us after all," Scot said to the others.

"You are making a wise decision here, Ms. Cambridge," Montgomery said to her. "Your future is ensured by being with us."

"Good," Diana replied. "I have no future in this place. My home has and always will be in Harlech on the streets where I was born."

"That is true, my dear," Montgomery agreed, waving a finger at her. "You have the mind of a true leader. Believe me, you will not regret this decision. Your life can finally begin again when you return home."

"I don't see why we should delay," Scot suggested. "The police in this town have given us trouble. It would be better if we evacuated before they close in on us."

"Very well," Montgomery replied. "Have my car brought in and have a word with Andrew to start the plane. We are to leave at once."

"I'll get him on the phone right away," Scot said, taking out his cellphone.

"Good," Montgomery responded, tapping his cane into the floor. "Do not worry, Ms. Cambridge. We will soon leave this land that has caused you many sorrows and return to Harlech. I believe Scot has made arrangements for you to live under his care and roof where you will be well kept after. The man has waited for this day for a long time – the day where he can welcome you into his home to treat you as the daughter he always saw you as."

"Thank you, sir," Diana replied. "I'm extremely grateful for all of this. I just want to go and leave though."

"And leave we will, my dear," Montgomery affirmed. "The government made a mistake in sending you here and let that be a lesson to you. The government cannot be trusted. She made both an error and displayed her callousness when she took you under her wing. She tried to make you a child of the liberal state, to be reliant on her, and we are here to set you free and be independent. The liberal world is an illiberal world. We do what we can to survive as a family, all of us, and we accept you into this family until death do any of us part."

"To Victory," a man cheered, raising his shot glass.

"To Victory," the others replied, raising their shot glasses.

Scot got off his cellphone and raised a shot glass after they had all drank. He then took a shot and set it on the table.

"We can leave in thirty minutes," Scot informed them. "I've had our cars come for us. Once we leave, it'll be about an hour flight back to Harlech."

"Good," Diana replied.

"Was that a taxi that just drove off in front of the manor?" Charlemagne questioned to himself, looking out of the curtains of his laboratory. "It was," he confirmed as it drove past again.

Charlemagne took off his goggles and set his screwdriver on his workbench. He then left his lab and went around to the second floor balcony of the library. He entered and looked down to where he saw Mavis dusting some shelves.

"Mr. Cabernet," Mavis greeted, stepping off the step-ladder she was on. "How can I be of service?"

"Where's Diana?"

"I have no clue," Mavis confessed. "I haven't seen her since breakfast."

"Where's my drone? I left her with the robot in this room. It was supposed to follow her and alert me if she left this room," Charlemagne complained, walking down the circular staircase to set foot on the ground floor. "Where are they?"

Charlemagne looked around and opened the windows of the library. He then began to search under desks and tables for his drone. He picked up the book Diana was reading, read the title as *The Brothers Karamazov* and then set it down. Charlemagne looked at the book and then continued to search around.

"I have no idea where on Earth she could have gone to," Mavis explained with an anxious look. "I didn't even know she was supposed to be in here."

"Quiet, please," Charlemagne said to her as he froze. "Do you hear that?"

The two listened and heard a buzzing noise of the rotors of the drone. Charlemagne walked around the room and then came to his knees. He looked under the grand piano in the corner of the room and saw his drone with a broken rotor, struggling to hover as it kept hitting the belly of the piano. Its camera was fixated on a picture frame.

"Oh, she is crafty," Charlemagne admitted, taking out the picture frame to see that it was a picture of her.

Charlemagne then picked up the drone as it started to beep ecstatically. Charlemagne quickly turned it off and then placed it atop of the piano. He then blew off the dust on the picture and brought it back to the table it was on.

"She's escaped to go to her race," Charlemagne explained, walking out of the library and into his study.

"Oh, dearie me," Mavis replied, following Charlemagne. "What can I do?"

"Nothing, love," Charlemagne responded, turning to her. "Please, stay here and look after Tristan until I return."

Charlemagne walked over to a telephone at his desk and then picked up a notepad with various phone numbers, including the non-emergency line for the Nattau County Police Department. He tracked the number of the equestrian center and dialed it.

"Barney Cohen," the owner of the equestrian center answered. "Who is this?"

"Cohen, it's Cabernet," Charlemagne replied. "Where is my daughter? Where is Diana?"

"Diana? How should I know where she is? I thought you grounded her like you told me?"

"Do not lie to me, you swine," Charlemagne barked. "If you do not tell me where she is, I'll have to police question you about it and consider this a matter of child abduction."

"Even if Diana were here, she would be here of her own accord, Charles," Barney replied in an impatient tone. "And if you call this number again, I'll consider it harassment. Goodnight."

Cohen hanged up on him, causing Charlemagne to slam the telephone down. He then left into the library.

"Diana!" Charlemagne called out. "Diana!"

Charlemagne entered the foyer and called her name again. No response came. He then walked upstairs and called her name again from the north wing foyer before going down the hall.

"Diana!"

Charlemagne stopped at her bedroom and opened the door. He looked around briefly before going into the bathroom, and through the bathroom into the gym where Tristan was. Tristan was working out with some dumbbells, sitting on his bench and curling the weights.

"Did you lose something?" Tristan remarked, looking at Charlemagne through the mirrors on the wall.

"Where's Diana? I know that you know," Charlemagne said, crossing his arms.

"I'm not giving her another reason to hate me," Tristan replied in a dull tone. "She's mad at me because she thinks I ratted on her about her being a jockey."

"You knew?!"

Tristan didn't reply.

"My God," Charlemagne remarked, uncrossing his arms and bringing his hands to his forehead. "All of this is maddening."

"You're overwhelmed," Tristan said. "Welcome to being a parent."

"I thought Diana went to the equestrian center, but her manager denied it. I don't know where else she could have gone."

"She'll turn up eventually…" Tristan replied. "Right? Maybe she went to the Medici Manor again."

"Perhaps," Charlemagne responded. "I'll phone the residence and try to talk to Dino. If they can't help us, I'm afraid this will have to be a matter for the police."

Charlemagne left the gym.

"The police?" Tristan questioned, standing up and following Charlemagne. "Why bring them into this? They'll complicate the matter. Not to mention, I'm sure Diana is peeved by them."

"I'm sorry, Tristan, but I considered that all this time and have been left with no choice."

Charlemagne went downstairs and to his study. Tristan rolled his eyes at the base of the stairs and then went back upstairs. He wiped his face with his grey t-shirt as he entered the gym again. From the gym, he walked into the bathroom and then into Diana's bedroom. He looked around and his eyes pointed at something on the ground in front of the French window. His eyes then looked at something atop of Diana's desk.

Tristan walked over to the sheet of paper and picked it up. He then read the note aloud:

"Dear Charles, I'm sorry for causing you so much grief ever since I came to this home of yours. I didn't intend for any of it, but I knew it was the type of burden I carried with me as I carried it with me to every foster home I was brought into. We lasted long together, but it was inevitable that we'd see conflict. We're different people, rich and poor. Even after you found that 'fourth level of happiness' you said you missed, and adopted me for sure, I still didn't feel a part of this home the way Tristan might say he does. I'll never fit in with you two because I'm too different. I enjoyed the adventure that you brought, but I don't think it's for me. Please, don't try to look for me because it would be a waste of time. I've left the county and province to go home with the syndicate. You might not trust them, but they're good people who have been there for me when nobody else was. This

is where I need to be and where my future lies – with them. Everything has lined up nicely, which leads me to think that this is how it should be. Arturo is going to school in Harlech. Zephyr, my horse, is in a nice home where he will be loved and cared for. You can stay with Tristan, without me to interfere, and I can go home and be with the people that understand me. It's all perfect. It's a perfect ending for all of us. Thanks for everything you've done. Best, Diana."

Tristan finished reading the letter and then sat it down. He had a tear coming down his eye.

"Yeah, I guess everybody is happy then," Tristan muttered. "Except me."

Tristan put the letter back on the desk and then walked over to see what was on the ground. He picked it up and saw pieces of glass drop down. He then looked at the picture of him and Diana in St. Petersburg and sat down on her bed. Tristan put the picture onto the bed and then buried his face into his hands. He then removed them and looked up.

"All of this started because I almost died," Tristan acknowledged. "It hurt her because I meant something to her. She doesn't really like Arturo, does she? She's just expressing herself to him because she can't with me. If she stays with him, she'll hurt him too and worse, herself. All of this... it's between her and me. Except, she thinks I betrayed her when I didn't. How do I prove myself otherwise? I need to stop her – I need to talk to her. I need to tell her how much I love her – I need to express how much I love her and show her."

Tristan stood up and picked up the letter. He took it with him and put it in the secret compartment in his desk before leaving. He then went downstairs to where he found Mavis in the kitchen.

"Mavis," Tristan said, "I need to go somewhere. Can you drive me?"

Mavis looked at Tristan from where she was cutting vegetables on a cutting board. She looked at Tristan who was dressed in black shorts, a grey t-shirt, and running shoes.

"Certainly," Mavis replied. "Where to?"

"I'll give you directions – it's a complicated place."

"Okay, certainly, Tristan," Mavis replied, washing her hands in the sink before drying them. "Let me just get my purse."

Mavis and Tristan walked into the supply closet and took the elevator down to the garage. She collected her purse before she went over to the black sedan, unlocked it and then opened the back door for Tristan. The two entered and then backed out to leave the manor through the garage. The car left the property and turned left onto the road.

Tristan saw police cars travelling towards the house from the off-ramp as they went forward to go across the bridge. He looked at them anxious before focusing in front of him as they went forward.

Act 6, Scene 3

Mavis drove to town and then turned to drive south towards the equestrian center. Tristan had her pull into the parking lot and wait for him as he ran inside. He passed through the lobby and made his way into the barn. There, he ran down the long corridor before he was stopped by a man exiting an office.

"Excuse me," the man spoke in an Irish accent. "Can I help you?"

Tristan turned and looked at him.

"Yeah, maybe you can," Tristan said to him. "I'm looking for one of your jockeys. I'm her brother, adopted-brother. Her name is Diana. Diana Cambridge. She rides…"

"Zephyr," the man replied. "I know her. Is she here?"

"No," Tristan responded, "but she was at home, and then she left a runaway letter and disappeared, and now I'm trying to find her because I know why she's upset – but she mentioned something about some criminals and I need to find them before it's too late. She's making a big mistake in leaving."

"Leaving?" the man replied, walking down the corridor with Tristan. "Where to?"

"Harlech," Tristan answered. "She's- she's upset at me because she loves me, and I love her, but she thinks I was the one that told our guardian that she was racing, but I wasn't. I don't know who it was, but it wasn't me. She's had an extremely bad week, and it's my fault that I wasn't there for her. I've been playing with her emotions even though I didn't mean to. I'm just- I'm weak and selfish. I'm a terrible person, but I need to stop her, please."

"Well…" the man sighed, "I thought she was here because a friend of hers arrived with her horse. They're in the central barn right now. Perhaps he can help you."

The two walked to the end of the corridor and came to a large door that slid up for them to pass into the barn. Sean and Tristan frowned as they saw what they did inside.

Several workers were attempting to hold Zephyr down with some ropes while Barney held a tranquilizer gun. In the background, Arturo was being held back by security guards.

"You lied to me!" Arturo shouted. "You said she would be here!"

"I need a clear shot!" Cohen yelled. "This stuff is expensive, so if I miss I'm hounding your asses!"

"We're trying," a worker grunted. "He's too tough!"

"What the hell is going on here!" Sean shouted. "Cohen, enough!"

"Oh crap!" a worker panicked as he turned to face Sean.

The worker lost control of his side of the rope and ran away. Zephyr got loose from the ropes and reared at the other workers. He neighed loudly and then stomped his hooves onto the metal ground before turning to face Barney.

"Whoa, easy there, big guy," Barney reasoned. "Remember me? I'm your uncle Barney."

The other workers lost control and began to run off as Sean stepped forward.

"Let go of me!" Arturo yelled.

"I don't believe this," Sean scolded, shaking his head. "Or perhaps I should."

Zephyr turned to his side and kicked Barney backwards. Tristan rushed over to calm Zephyr, waving his hands at him.

"Easy there," Tristan said to him. "Easy, look at me."

The horse looked at Tristan and approached him.

"Oh, God..." Barney complained, hands at his torso. "I think- I think I broke everything."

Sean ran over to him and checked him. Barney ripped open his shirt where it was red.

"How long have you been cheating during this derby?" Sean questioned. "You promised me you'd stop!"

"Call an ambulance," Cohen begged, grabbing Sean's shirt. "Please."

"Answer me!"

Arturo broke loose from the grip of security and sucker punched one of the guards onto the ground. The other panicked and ran off from him. Arturo then ran over to stop Zephyr from getting too close to Tristan.

"What are you doing here? What is *he* doing here? Diana said that she left Zephyr in proper care," Tristan said to him.

"She meant me, dumbass," Arturo replied. "And what do you mean she talked to you? Isn't she mad at you?"

"She is, but she left a note on her desk explaining how she was going to run away and join up with some syndicate she knows. She wants to go to Harlech to be with you and them."

"Wait, what?" Arturo questioned.

"What are you doing here with Zephyr?" Tristan asked.

"I thought Diana was going to come and race her final race," Arturo replied. "I even got a call from this parasite over here, asking me about Diana and telling me to bring the horse over, but I was duped."

"Yeah, and how'd that work out?" Tristan replied with a bitter tone.

"You're the reason she's ran off!" Arturo yelled at him. "What is wrong with you?"

"Nothing," Tristan replied.

"Enough!" Sean yelled at them before turning to Barney. "How long has this been going on?"

"Forever," Barney finally confessed. "I never stopped after we shook on it."

"You mean, you were responsible for Bell Bell's dosage?"

"No," Barney replied. "I'm better than that. The horses are being injected with a new substance that is undetectable by current standards of testing. All the horses in the last race had it except Bell Bell because the idiot manager thought he was being smart by using an older version of the drug."

"You hook-nosed idiot!" Sean cursed at him. "You doped those horses so they could win, didn't' you? You knew that everybody would bet on Zephyr winning, so you rigged the match against them. She was right!"

"Please, I made so much money, I just- I can't help it."

"You are pathetic," Sean said, shaking his head at him. "I'll call your ambulance, but they'll be with police to take you in afterwards."

Barney began to cry as he hugged himself. Sean stood up and looked over to the boys.

"We need to find Diana before she leaves," Sean said.

"Do you have any idea who these syndicate people are?" Tristan asked Arturo.

"Not really," Arturo replied, "but my cousin Dino might know. If they're in Allabrese, we would have been keeping track of them. I'll give him a call."

Arturo took out his phone and called Dino while Tristan looked at Sean.

"Do you know what you're going to say to her when you find her?" Sean asked.

"Partially," Tristan replied, "but I don't want to just speak words. I want to express myself. It's difficult. I didn't realize how hard this is. I thought I could just be with them and that would be enough."

"Being with a woman is more than just being with them. It's about being there for them and taking care of them. You need to be a man to be with a woman, and that includes defending her, standing up for yourself and her and being strong because to love a woman requires that you be passionate about her and able to express this and talk to her about everything in your life and every emotion you experience, because they enjoy the attention and most importantly, they care about us and want to be included in our lives. Likewise, because they are passionate about you. It's more about being their friends. It's about being their partner in life to be able to raise children together in confidence and in a relationship for which these children will learn of primarily and come to model their future relationships after."

"So, what do I do?" Tristan asked.

Sean rolled his eyes.

"Express your passion for her if you have any. If not, now is the time to find your passion in Diana, which I can see already seeing that you're here and want to find her. However, I must caution your motive. If you are really here for her, then go find her. If you are here for yourself because you treat Diana like an object of pleasure, then it would be better for her to love and let the other boy go find her."

"No!" Tristan refused. "Diana's angst is between me and her. I want to believe that I'm being selfless in wanting to stop her from ruining her life, but I can feel my own motives within me."

"All natural love has a degree of selfishness, but as long as you are mindful and remember not to treat your woman like an object, then you are fine."

"I don't want to treat her like a pet or an object. I want to treat her right."

"I know where she is!" Arturo yelled. "Dino said he's tracked some suspicious British businessmen throughout Allabrese and that they've been spotted at the airfield with a plane."

Tristan looked back at Sean as Arturo came over to them.

"I have to go after her," Tristan said to them. "I'm the only one that can talk her out of this."

"Diana's angry at you because you betrayed her," Arturo said to him.

"She's also angry because she's uncertain about me," Tristan added. "She doesn't know for sure if I betrayed her because Charlemagne's wording was so damn vague. She's uncertain about whether she can trust me, but I'll talk to her. I'm going to be there for her and rescue her. I'm going to make this right."

Tristan took a step back before Arturo stopped him. Arturo had approached Tristan and put a hand on his shoulder.

"I'll stay here then," Arturo said. "Talk to her and make this right with her, but if you fail let me know so I can talk to her. I'll talk to Dino and see about them sending some backup to you. Do you have a way of getting over there?"

"Uh, not really…" Tristan replied before looking over to Zephyr.

"I think someone wants to help you," Sean remarked, looking at Zephyr who was following Tristan.

Tristan looked at Zephyr who was looking intently at Tristan. He had his reins in his mouth and dropped them on the ground. Tristan walked over and picked them up.

"Alright, let's go rescue Diana then," Tristan said, putting the reins on the horse before mounting him. "I'll text you if I fail."

"Sure thing," Arturo replied.

"Good luck, kid," Sean said as Tristan started to ride into the closed pasture. "Godspeed."

Tristan rode along the grass and made his approach to the fencing. Zephyr hopped over the fence and then continued towards the road at Tristan's direction. The sun was still in the sky but beginning to set behind the Rocky Mountains in the west. Zephyr galloped towards the river bridge and then northwest towards the airfield.

On their approach, Tristan could see the large cargo plane on the runway with its turbines roaring. The rear cargo door was open and there were men in white dress shirts and black dress pants pulling jacks into the plane with cargo. Behind Tristan, on the road, vintage black cars began to speed along and come to the airport. They crossed into the airfield and parked at the start of the runway. Medici gang members in blue suits rushed out and took cover behind their cars as Tristan arrived to join them.

Tristan disembarked at the lead car where he saw Dino Medici. The two gangs found themselves in a gunfight as Tristan took cover.

"I'm glad you're here," Tristan said to Dino.

"How could we resist?" Dino replied, reloading a magazine into his pistol. "We're a one mafia county. The last thing that the Medici family does is share."

"Help me get Diana off the plane before they take off," Tristan briefed. "We can't let them takeoff."

"No problem," Dino responded. "We'll put as much fire against them as we can, but there's no guarantee that they'll – damn! They're taking off! You better be quick! We'll keep opening fire on them."

Tristan looked over as he saw the gunfire stop from the opposing side. The plan started to move forward with the cargo doors hovering over the tarmac.

"We'll pursue from behind. Keep clear of the turbines!" Dino shouted. "Move!"

Tristan mounted Zephyr again and made his way forward and behind the rear cargo door. The Medici gang members began to drive along the sides of the plane, keeping clear from the turbines. Syndicate enforcers started to fire back at Tristan, causing him to have to steer clear. After the Medici cars got in position, they started to open fire against the side of the plane. The gunfire from inside stopped.

The syndicate enforcers started to push crates down the ramp. Tristan dodged them and started to see the doors rising up to close. He pushed Zephyr to go faster, coming to the side of the ramp and climbing up onto the back of Zephyr so he could place a hand on the side. He grabbed ahold and then was pulled off from Zephyr. He pulled himself up and then slid down the side to land inside the rear of the plane.

Inside, there was a mere red light providing guidance for the whole of the crowded cargo hold. Tristan hid behind a crate and could hear bullets tapping the sides of the hull. He moved out from where he was taking cover and rushed around some boxes, evading the gangsters around. He reached the back of the cargo hold where there was a small ladder going up into a corridor into the depths of the plane.

"Stowaway!" a British-accented voice yelled from behind.

Tristan climbed the ladder but was suddenly tackled backwards by a figure that rushed towards him through the darkness. The figure was atop of him. He blocked a punch from the figure and felt her soft hands. The figure let go and Tristan moved his hands out of the way so he could see. Diana stopped herself from punching Tristan as they eyes met and she could make out Tristan's face through the red light.

"Tristan?" Diana questioned, panting lightly.

The other enforcers encircled them with guns drawn out. Diana realized this and quickly got off from Tristan and raised her palms to them.

"Stop," Diana pleaded. "He's not our enemy."

Diana then looked down at Tristan.

"What the hell are you doing here?" Diana questioned.

"I'm here for you," Tristan replied. "I- I found your note, and I didn't want you to make a mistake in leaving. Diana, it's my fault you're upset and rightfully so, but I swear on my parents' grave that I didn't tell Charlemagne about the race. Look, here are texts between us that show I didn't tell him when he asked me moments beforehand. It's not much, but it's all I have to try and convince you that I've been honest."

Diana took Tristan' phone from him and looked at the messages.

"The reason I'm leaving is more than just our fight," Diana replied, giving him his phone back.

"But I'm the root of your problems," Tristan responded to her. "I've been a terrible person to you ever since I fell through that ice and you saved my life, and I'm sorry. I don't want you to leave though, because I love you. Running away isn't going to solve anything because you love me too and you'll only burn yourself up and punish those around you, including Arturo with these burnt up feelings between us."

"Tristan…" Diana grunted, feeling embarrassed.

"I'll always be there for you, Diana. I'll never leave your side. I'll always be there to climb onto a moving plane and come for you. I'll always be there when you need a shoulder to cry on until you tell me to stop and go away, because I love you and my heart is yours and only yours. Even then, I'll still be there for you."

Diana blushed as Tristan stood up. He walked over to her and offered his hand.

"Please, come home with me," Tristan proposed. "You don't have to be upset over me anymore. I'm here for you and I love you. If coming across town, climbing onto an airplane, and telling you all this in front of a bunch of thugs isn't a sign that I love you, then I don't know what is. I've done everything else. I've told you how I feel and opened myself up to you, what more?"

Diana looked at him and then his hand.

"If you didn't snitch on me, then who did? Who told Charlemagne about my race?"

"I told him," a Scottish voice said from behind.

Diana turned around and saw Scot come towards them with a pistol in-hand.

"I told the old man that you were racing and sent him various documents to try and convince him to hand you over to us."

"What?" Diana questioned to him. "How could you?"

"Because you belong in our care, Diana. You are a special woman with talent and of noble descent," Scot explained. "Even if your father was a terrible man, he was still your father and the son of greater people who suffered. You didn't deserve that life, and it's been our intentions to bring you into the organization when you were old enough. Ever since you stole from me, I was assigned to watch over you and protect you. When I saw you at the airport in January, I thought I had a chance to rescue you myself. I wanted to give you the home you deserved."

"So, you're the reason that Charlemagne knew…" Diana said, looking back over to Tristan apologetically.

"Yes," Scot confirmed. "I'm sorry for any hardships it may have forced upon you, but it was what I needed to do. I don't expect you to understand that."

"No, I do understand, but I'm not happy about it," Diana replied.

"Don't you see still though? You are better off in Harlech, Diana. Do you understand that too? Scot questioned.

Diana didn't reply.

"Harlech is a place with a lot of nostalgia, and I spent both good and bad days there," Diana remarked. "I don't know if I would be any happier there now than I was here when I started to live with Tristan and get used to Allabrese."

Scot pointed his gun towards Tristan. Diana was immediately alerted by this, stepped back and took Tristan's hand.

"Please, don't shoot him," Diana pleaded, keeping Tristan behind her. "Scot, all of what you said is ideal. I would have wanted to be your daughter and be raised by you. I consider you as a father-figure, but- but I do love Tristan. I'd be worse off in Harlech apart from him because I'd miss him and there would be undisclosed feelings between us. Allabrese is my home now. With him. I'm old enough to be away from home, from my father, and if your reasoning is that I need protection, then I thank you for the offer, but Tristan will protect me."

Scot continued to point the gun at the two of them with trembling hands. He focused the muzzle of his gun towards him.

"If you want to shoot, then shoot him. I've stated what I want, and if you want to go behind me then you'll have to shoot through me," Diana declared. "Go ahead, shoot."

Scot held the gun pointed, closed his eyes and brought his finger to the trigger. He then opened his eyes and relaxed his finger away from the trigger.

"Fine," Scot sighed, lowering his gun. "If you can tell the gangsters outside to stand down, then you're free to go. I can't coerce you, Diana. I can't shoot him either. You love him. You know the truth about my intentions, and you're at your own right to decide as you said. I shouldn't have lied to you, especially since I claim to consider you to be my own daughter."

Scot put his pistol in his holster.

"I want the best for you, Diana. I thought that would be with us in the organization, but I see now that there is a better and alternative path to that, which I approve. You deserve this kind of happiness after what you've been though – what your father put you through. All I want is for you to come out better than him, and I trust that you'll do that on your own."

Scot turned around and walked away from them. The plane started to slow down. Diana walked with Tristan to the rear of the plane. Diana hit a switch to the lower the doors, and the two then walked out and towards the Medici gang members.

"You can stand down and go home," Tristan said to them.

Dino nodded and told the others to leave. Zephyr approached them as soon as he saw Diana. The gangsters got into their cars and then left. After they left, Diana hugged Tristan in a tight embrace.

"You better have meant what you said to me," Diana said in a muffled voice as her face was covered by Tristan's shirt.

"I meant every word of it," Tristan replied. "You don't have to take my word for it though."

Once Zephyr joined them, the two separated and were joined by enforcers of the syndicate as well as Scot. Diana turned to him.

"Thank you, Scot," Diana said as she held Tristan's hand. "I'll never forget all that you've done for me. I owe you twice now."

"What was the first favor? The pistol I gave you?" Scot questioned. "I considered that a present for you."

"No, I meant that *other* favor. Remember? You were the ones that killed my dad. I've always been grateful for that."

"Where did you hear that we killed him?" Scot questioned. "We- we never killed him."

"What?" Diana replied. "I was so sure that you did!"

"No," Scot answered, "your father was lousy at what he did, but we would never have killed him. Both your father and his partner were killed in separate incidents on the same night. We thought it was targeted against them, but we also suspected that Morris, your dad's partner, was plotting to kill him."

"Are you serious?"

"I'm serious. We investigated it and weren't able to find the true murderer. The death of your father is truly an unsolved mystery, but he had a target on his back since he upset so many people over the years. He made a lot of enemies."

"Huh…" Diana replied.

"Anyways, I'm glad we could talk about that," Scot said. "We have to leave now before the police show up too. If you're ever in Harlech again, please give me a call so we can catch up. Until then, take care. And you," he added, pointing at Tristan. "Take care of her with your life. Do you understand?"

"Yes, sir," Tristan agreed, nodding.

"Thanks, Scot. I'll see you around," Diana replied, waving goodbye.

The hull of the door closed behind them as they entered their plane. Diana, Tristan and Zephyr then came to the parking lot of the airfield so they could watch the plane takeoff. Diana tilted her head on Tristan's shoulder under the twilight of the night.

"What now?" Diana asked.

"Well, you still have a race to win," Tristan said to her.

"Should I even go? Is there even time?" Diana questioned. "Charlemagne wouldn't be happy… does he know I tried to run off?"

"He's the one that told me, and he called the cops," Tristan replied, "but if we go to the race, we don't have to explain all of this to him and just say that we were at the equestrian center."

"Good idea," Diana agreed. "Let's go."

Act 6, Scene 4

Tristan rode Zephyr back to the Allabrese Equestrian Center with Diana behind her, holding on. The horse jumped over the fences of the enclosure and then galloped to the opening in the barn. There, Sean was with Arturo.

"Oh, thank God you made it," Sean exclaimed, uncrossing his arms.

"Am I too late?" Diana questioned.

"You have twenty minutes to go and get changed," Sean said to her. "Your uniform and gear are in your dressing room."

"Where's Barney?" Tristan asked.

"On a stretcher and on his way to Allabrese Hospital," Sean explained.

"What?" Diana questioned.

"I'll explain on the way," Tristan said to her as they went down the stable corridor with Zephyr.

Tristan briefly explained that Barney was trying to dope Zephyr, but that he and Sean stopped him and in the process, Barney was kicked the in the chest and needed rapid transport to a hospital for possible hypovolemic shock.

"Here," Diana said, pointing to her dressing room.

"I'll go get Zephyr ready and then meet you back here," Tristan said as they stopped.

"Thank you," Diana replied, kissing him on the cheek. "There's a plaque where his stall is. It's not too far from here."

Diana hopped off and entered her dressing room while Tristan went down to find Zephyr's pen. Tristan readied Zephyr with his saddle and uniform. He then led him out and back to the dressing room where Diana was exiting.

"You look…"

"What?" Diana interrupted.

"Great," Tristan finished.

The three of them returned to the barn in line with the other horses. The barn was crowded, but they managed to find Sean who was alone. Tristan hopped off of Zephyr and passed the rein to Diana.

"Alright, we're ready," Tristan said to Sean.

"Good, and just on time too."

Horses were called out onto the track to approach the gate one-by-one in alphabetical order of the provinces. Drop Down was first out of the barn before Zephyr was lined up to go next.

"Whatever happens out there, everything will be fine," Sean said to Diana. "Good luck, Diana."

"Give them hell, city girl," Tristan added, smiling to her.

Diana smiled back.

"Next up, we have our second representative for our very own wild rose country. Ladies and gentlemen, give it up for Zephyr and his owner, Diana Cambridge from Allabrese," the P.A. announcer announced.

Diana led Zephyr out. Tristan and Sean walked with her to the gate.

"Diana was rumored to be missing earlier, but I suppose those were just rumors as here she is," the announcer added.

Cameras flashed and the crowd cheered for her. Across the sidelines there were various television crews, TV cameras, and journalists and photographers watching them. The four of them went to the gate and were followed by a spotlight that disappeared towards the gate so they could get ready. The announcer carried on with the other representatives from other provinces.

After Sean helped Diana into the cage, he went off to the sidelines with Tristan. Tristan looked around the crowd briefly before looking back to the gates.

"And here we are, folks," the announcer proclaimed. "The grand finale of the Nattau Derby – the championship race. We have twenty competitors, two from each province, and only one first place position and cup to give away. Who will win? We're about to find out."

Diana steadied herself and stroked Zephyr's neck. She then stopped to tighten her grip on the reins and take deep breaths.

"Let's do this," Diana whispered to Zephyr.

The bell rang and the gates swung open.

"And it's go!" the announcer yelled.

The horses launched from their cages and started the race. All twenty of them stomped their way forward and gravitated towards the inner perimeter of the track, pushing each other as most of them formed a herd with stragglers behind and two in the lead. Zephyr was stuck in the middle of the crowd on the first stretch.

"Here we go! We have Clip Clop moving forward into first place, and behind them is Compass pushing along to challenge them. Helium sticks out as she leads the crowd in third. Oh- Helium is passed by Drop Down.

Diana felt the other horses bumping against Zephyr as they all raced towards the first turn. Zephyr started to slow down as they made the turn.

"Zephyr moves along to the back of the central mob. Drop Down takes the lead at three lengths from Compass and Clip Clop," the announcer updated.

"Come on, Zeph," Diana said. "We don't need steroids to kick ass. We can do this."

Zephyr continued to gallop ahead in a light pace. He began to speed up as they approached the second turn. The horses in the lead held a good distance from them and were already finishing the second turn.

Diana began to guide Zephyr away from the herd and steered him around them. He then sped up and proceeded to pass them.

"Oh, looks like Zephyr is picking up the pace and is going for fifth," the announcer said. "Drop Down is still four lengths ahead though with Compass, Clip Clop, and Helium behind."

Zephyr stomped forward and led the herd before pushing forward during the stretch to the third turn. They maintained their position as they started to turn and come for the fourth turn.

"Almost there," Diana said to Zephyr. "We're almost there."

Zephyr fastened his pace and stormed forward towards the horse in fourth, passing them and then making their approach to third place as they started to turn. Zephyr continued to accelerate and leave these horses behind before going even faster than before.

"Zephyr is *really* kicking into gear as he passes not only Helium and Compass but is also making his way towards Clop Clop and Drop Down. It's coming close, folks!"

At the approach to the turn, Zephyr passed Clip Clop. He then homed in on Drop Down ahead.

"My God, I never thought I could see a horse gallop so fast," the announcer awed. "Drop Down has a good lead, but will Zephyr overtake him in these last yards?"

"Easy, bud," Diana said to Zephyr as they came closer to Drop Down. "Easy…"

The jockey riding Drop Down turned around and then looked forward. He took his whip and started to slap the horses ass to go faster.

"Go!" Diana said to Zephyr. "Go!"

Zephyr pushed ahead and started to come to the side of the other jockey at the last stretch. Zephyr proceeded forward with a boost that pushed them ahead after the final turn.

"Zephyr takes Drop Down. Drop Down takes Zephyr. Oh! Zephyr takes Drop Down again, and… he's not stopping. Ladies and gentlemen, Zephyr is not stopping even as Drop Down tries to overtake them! Zephyr takes the lead and is going home with a good length, no two lengths! Four?!"

"She's going to do it," Tristan whispered.

"I've never seen a horse ride that fast," Sean remarked.

"Zephyr is at six lengths ahead of second-place and is riding towards the finish line!" the announcer updated. "The cavalry rush behind him as they cross the final hundred meter mark. It doesn't matter though because Zephyr has crossed and taken first place! That's it! Zephyr wins the cup! Oh my Lord, that must have been a new record! I've never seen a race end so quickly!"

Zephyr had passed the finish line and slowed down at Diana's lead. The two continued to gallop ahead for a victory lap while the other horses finished behind them.

"Zephyr does it, folks! Zephyr and Diana have beaten their competition in a stunning comeback. Drop Down finishes in second place with Clip Clop at third, Compass in fourth, and Helium in fifth. Ladies and gentlemen, that concludes the seventy-seventh annual Nattau Derby. What an ending too…"

Diana came back around and slowed down as she led Zephyr towards the sidelines. Cameras flashed towards her as she took Zephyr to receive their prize. A heavily decorated garland was placed around Zephyr's neck and Diana was given a bouquet of local flowers as well as a gold-plated trophy with a horse rearing on the top. Diana also shook the hands of the derby officials and then took her picture with them and Sean.

Diana and Zephyr took many pictures and stood-by. Tristan watched from behind with a light smile, looking at Diana with her large smile.

"Am I too late for the race?" an English-accented voice said from the side.

Tristan looked over and saw Charlemagne walk over with Arturo. In Charlemagne's hands, he held something – a book.

"Yeah…" Tristan replied, "but you're not too late to see her be happy."

"Thank you, Arturo, for telling me that she was here," Charlemagne said, watching on before turning to Tristan. "I was sure to notify the police that we found her."

"They arrested Barney," Tristan informed him. "I thought you'd be happy about that."

"I couldn't care less," Charlemagne remarked. "On my way here, I was contemplating how I would handle punishing her for this, but to be honest, mistakes have been made from all of us. I just need to remain authoritative, but not careless – assertive, but not authoritarian."

"You're new to all of this," Tristan added. "It's okay. We love you the same."

Charlemagne sighed.

"I thought I had lost her for good. I thought she might have ran off to go home to Harlech, and when I learned she was here, I felt a relief that at least she was still in the county and mildly safe."

Charlemagne then sighed again.

"Thank you, Tristan, for getting her back for me."

"How did you know I did this?"

"Because I trusted you to do the right thing," Charlemagne confessed. "Come, she's breaking away from the crowd."

The three of them walked along the perimeter of the track and met up with Diana, Sean and Zephyr away from the crowds of people. Diana had dismounted from Zephyr and was simply walking with him.

"Charles…" Diana said as she looked at Charlemagne.

"Hello, Diana," Charlemagne responded in a calm tone. "I believe I owe you an apology for being too hard on you. All of this parenting is new to me, and… I never had parents of my own to learn from. Please, forgive me."

"I'm sorry too," Diana confessed. "I can take blame in all this too."

Diana saw what Charlemagne was holding in his hands. He presented it to her.

"I found this in the library and knew it was yours," Charlemagne remarked, passing her the copy of *The Brothers Karamazov*. "I thought it to be a little too advanced for you to understand, but then again, I know what kind of childhood you had and the type of father you had to make you perhaps see Alyosha's father, Fyodor, to be like your own. In truth, when I first read this book, that's what I saw as well."

Sean proceeded to lead Zephyr back indoors. Tristan and Arturo joined them as they left Charlemagne with Diana.

"We may have lived and grown up in different economic conditions," Charlemagne continued, "but both of us had similar parents. My father was negligent, careless, and abusive with me. I'm not too sure what yours was like, but by the tone you speak of him, I can only imagine the worst. In contrast, my mother was caring and warm."

"Mine too…" Diana replied, looking down.

"My parents may be alive, but it doesn't mean I don't know what yours were like or what you might be experiencing. When I found this book on the table, I didn't think of all this at first, but instead of myself because I knew I was doing a poor job being your adoptive-father. I have no excuse for that behavior because it was my behavior and mine alone, but I do hope to improve and be a better guardian in the future if you can understand that this is new to me."

"You don't have to apologize, Charles," Diana replied. "You're new to being a father of a teenager, and I'm new to being a teenager and a daughter to an inexperienced father. We can just learn from this and try not to repeat it."

"I'm glad you are understanding," Charlemagne responded, walking with her. "You're a bright girl, Diana."

"Thank you."

"Come now," Charlemagne said as they continued to walk, "I won't keep you from your celebrations. Congratulations on your victory – it was well-deserved."

The two entered the barn and then went down the stable corridor to her dressing room. Diana entered and put her flowers and book there. Sean had brought in the trophy and was opening a bottle of champagne.

"Celebrate with me, Mr. Cabernet," Sean said to him as he entered.

"Where's Arturo? Tristan?" Diana questioned.

"Arturo said he had to leave, and Tristan is taking Zephyr to his pen," Sean explained.

Diana left and went down the corridor to the stable. She met Tristan there.

"Hey," Diana said to him.

"Oh, hey," Tristan replied, smiling at her. "Congratulations, you've out-horsed me."

"You know that was my intention all along," Diana sarcastically remarked, smiling at her. "Wait for me in the dressing room. I have to go talk to Arturo before he leaves."

"Okay…" Tristan replied.

"You can come with me if you want," Diana invited.

"Are you sure?"

"I don't want you to be suspicious or to get jealous."

"Jealous? Me?" Tristan questioned. "Nah, you go ahead."

"Okay," Diana smiled at him. "I won't be long."

Diana left and ran down the corridor to the main lobby of the sports center. She then rushed to the front entrance and caught Arturo on the sidewalk, sitting down at the curb and smoking.

"Hey," Diana said to him, "thanks for helping out."

"It's no problem," Arturo replied. "I was glad to be a part of it."

Diana walked over and sat down next to him.

"Is everything cool with you and Tristan then?" Arturo questioned.

"Yeah, everything is cool and better," Diana replied.

"I'm glad," Arturo replied. "You know, ever since you told me about him at school, I knew I had no chance. I didn't really care even though I like you. I believed you deserved the best, and what you have with Tristan is something we'd never be able to have."

"Why did you ask for my permission to go to Harlech?"

"I wanted to know what you'd decide, and I'm pleased you let me go," Arturo said to her. "To be honest, I've enjoyed these last couple of months together, and I needed them to heal from what happened to me and what I did. I didn't deserve any of this though considering what I did."

"Don't say that," Diana replied.

"No, it's true. I'm not saying that I don't deserve to find someone and find love like you and Tristan have, nor do I want to at this moment. I have my dream to fulfill and that's all I look forward to at the moment. It's what motivates me. One day, I'll find someone, but I'll leave it to fate to decide when that happens – when I'm to meet a woman that impresses me as much as you have. Until then, I only have one thing to ask from you…"

"What's that?" Diana asked as Arturo looked to her.

"Live on and fulfill your dream, Diana. I hope you and Tristan together are what needs to happen for both of you to fulfill your purpose and dreams, that way, we all move forward. I know the two of you will be together for a long time. Maybe until death do you part, because you have a strong connection and he's passionate about you. He does love you. Never forget that."

Arturo stood up as a car came for him. She stood up after him. He put out his cigarette and then turned to Diana.

"Never forget that," Arturo said again. "God has given you Tristan. Love him as the Church, the communion of believers, loves Christ, Diana. Never forget that God loves you and that you are His daughter as well."

Arturo entered the car and then closed the door. Diana watched as the car drove off. She then walked back inside and returned to the stables. She walked down the corridor and stopped in the pen where Tristan was with Zephyr still.

"Wow, that was quick," Tristan said to her. "Is everything okay?"

"Everything is fine," Diana replied. "I just said my goodbye to him, and you know what? I feel happy for him. He's going to be alright."

"Everything is going to be alright," Tristan added in his optimistic tone.

Tristan took Diana's hands and looked at her. The two kissed and then parted as Zephyr interrupted them and huffed in their ears.

"Zephyr…" Diana laughed before hugging him. "You jealous boy."

Tristan laughed and the three of them hugged together. They then parted from the horse and left him behind to join the others.

Diana and Tristan held hands as they walked down the corridor, taking their time to reach the dressing room. Diana smiled as Tristan let go and put his left arm around her. The couple walked together with passionate smiles on their faces as they were together.

Epilogue

Charlemagne tapped the papers in his hands against his desk as he looked to the TV above the fireplace in his study. It was displaying a documentary on Ancient Egypt.

"Egypt is better known as the Land of the Pharaohs," the narrator described before the TV was turned off.

Charlemagne placed the remote to the TV on his desk and then walked over to the cabinet on the left from his desk chair. He crouched and placed the papers in his hand, titled 'Harlech Syndicate Report on Diana Cambridge,' and slipped them into an envelope. He then tied the clip around the envelope and placed it inside of a safe at the bottom of the cabinet. He then closed the cabinet door and then walked to exit his study, turning off the light behind him.

●

Tristan opened his eyes and looked ahead of him in the darkness of Diana's bedroom. He had his arm wrapped around Diana's waist and the back of her head in front of him. The two of them were in bed. Diana began to shiver and moan. Tristan brought the covers up to cover her some more. He then hugged her and brought her closer to him.

"Hey, it's okay," Tristan whispered. "I'm here with you, Diana."

Tristan held on to her and took a deep breath. He closed his eyes. Diana began to whine again.

"Easy," Tristan said to her in a soothing voice. "Everything is okay."

Diana calmed down and gave a deep exhale. Tristan gave a sigh of relief and loosened his grip on her. He then closed his eyes and drifted into a deep sleep, sticking by her side throughout the night and nights to come ever more.

"The man that lives in a small community lives in a much larger world."

– G.K. Chesterton